THE ITALIAN FAKE DATE

a large print, sweet romance full
of heart and family, set in Italy

Stefania Hartley

The Sicilian Mama

This title was first published as "Her Mother's Secret" by The People's Friend.

Cover illustration and design by Joseph Witchall

https://josephwitchall.com/

CHAPTER 1

The last place left to clear in her parents' house was the loft and Alice wasn't looking forward to it at all. It was bound to bring back lots of memories and reignite her grief.

She couldn't keep her parents' home as a shrine forever, however. Two years had passed since the motorbike accident that had claimed their lives. It was time to let go of the house and let other people make their home there.

As a single woman in her twenties with a receptionist job in a busy London hotel, she didn't need a family-size home in the countryside.

And the way her love life had been going so far, she wouldn't need it any time soon.

She opened the loft hatch and a wall of hot air tumbled over her. She pulled down the ladder and climbed up.

The attic was stifling hot and dusty. She turned on the torch her father always kept by the entrance, trying not to recall that he had been the last person to touch it.

As she had expected, the loft was full of memories: toys from her childhood; suitcases from family holidays; and her parents' wedding clothes. It took a superhuman effort not to well up.

Tucked away in a cobwebbed corner was a small chest she had never seen before. It looked like somewhere to store treasure. Could it contain her parents' love letters? Some romantic first gifts? They had been very private people who rarely talked about themselves and kept their feelings close to their chests. They wouldn't like her reading their love letters.

Alice couldn't resist. Finding out new things about her mother and father felt as if they were still alive, still communicating with her.

She crouched down in front of the chest, dusted it with her hands and lifted the lid.

The first things she saw were a pink baby's jumpsuit and a baby blanket. These things weren't her parents' mementos, but hers!

Why had they never shown it to her? She had very few things from her babyhood and she would have loved to see these.

She lifted the blanket and stroked it against her cheeks. It was soft and smelled of baby powder. The jumpsuit was so cute!

Underneath were letters. The envelopes were addressed to her mother and had been stamped in Italy. Alice unfolded the first letter.

Dear Clare,

I hope that you read this letter and reply to me. I don't know whether you've received my previous letters. If you have, I hope you don't mind me writing again.

Please, understand that I don't regret giving you baby Francesca. I know that you will give her everything I can't.

I don't want to take her away from you. All I'm asking is news of her. It would make me so happy if you could send me a photo every now and then.

I promise that is all I want and that I won't make any trouble for you. I just miss ~~my~~ your baby.

Love,

Simona.

So the baby things weren't hers after all. Who was baby Francesca?

Perhaps she had fostered babies

before having Alice.

She read the letter again but it made no more sense than before. She opened the other letters but the content was the same: an Italian woman called Simona wanted news of her baby.

Alice put the letters aside and continued searching the box. Under a baby rattle and teething ring was an official-looking document, an adoption certificate. Could it belong to the people who had lived in the house before them?

Alice read the document carefully but the words made no sense. Her parents' names were in there. It wasn't true—it couldn't be. Alice Baker was her and she wasn't adopted.

Or was she? The names and dates on the document swam before her eyes.

She sank on her haunches and sat on the floor. The heat and the dust were choking her.

This was her adoption certificate. Baby Francesca was her.

CHAPTER 2

Paolo read the email from Gus one more time and sank on to the bed of his rented London room. The man wanted sketches of the artwork—a reasonable request—but Paolo had nothing to show him.

Not even the germ of an idea.

A much-respected art collector, Gus Le Boutton could make or break Paolo's career. Landing even the smallest art commission from Gus would have been a privilege. Being asked to create a sculpture for his wedding as a gift to his new bride was a huge honour, a once-in-a-lifetime chance to shine.

But Paolo's creative well had run dry.

The sculptures he had made for Rosaria, which had so impressed Gus, had come from the heart of a very different man from the Paolo today; a man who believed in love.

He had accepted Gus's commission —he would have been mad not to—but as time passed, he was less and less confident he could deliver the piece in time.

His Muse had abandoned him as heartlessly as had Rosaria.

His phone rang and he feared it might be Gus chasing him. His heart sank.

Thankfully, it was Lia, his mother.

"Hi, Mamma."

"Hi, love, how are you? Are you eating properly?"

Paolo smiled. Even though he worked in an Italian restaurant, his mother worried he might not have enough to eat.

"Yes, Mamma, I am."

"Are you all packed?"

"For what?"

"Coming home for your brother's wedding."

Silence hung between them. His brother, Marcello, was marrying Rosaria, the woman Paolo had dated for ten years and had planned to marry himself.

"You expect me to attend this wedding?"

"You still love Rosaria, then."

"I don't."

"Then why not come?"

"I haven't forgiven my brother."

"Oh, dear, oh, dear," she whispered.

Was that worse than still being in love with his future sister-in-law?

"Please, darling, forgive Marcello. It's not his fault. The heart doesn't obey orders. If they had fallen in love with each other, what could they do about it? Thankfully, they discovered it before you and Rosaria got married."

"I understand, Mamma. I just don't want my nose rubbed in it."

"You can't miss your brother's wedding. Your father and I will be very sad— and your brother, too, I'm sure. What's more, everyone in Altavicia will guess that you haven't forgiven him."

Paolo had never cared about what his fellow villagers thought but he cared very much about upsetting his parents.

They had done nothing wrong and they were heartbroken about the situation between him and his brother.

For his parents' sake, he could not shun Marcello and Rosaria's wedding.

Besides, a visit home was well overdue.

Since coming to London to study at the Royal Academy of Arts, he hadn't been back to Italy once.

What if a visit home were to get him out of his creative rut and inspire him to create Gus's sculpture? He could hole up in his artist's hut up on the mountains behind Altavicia and let nature be a balm to his soul and inspiration for his mind.

Yes, he decided, his best chance to recover his creativity was to return to his beautiful Calabria.

"Okay, Mamma. I'll come to Marcello's wedding."

CHAPTER 3

After her surprise discovery in the loft, Alice called in sick at work and spent the next two days in bed. The news of her adoption had floored her.

She called her best friend, who turned up with a tub of ice-cream and a selection of new nail polish.

"Would you like your nails glittery, pearly, matte or studded with stones?" Rachel asked, sitting on the chair next to Alice's bed.

"Sorry, I'm not in the mood," she muttered.

"Then you must be in the mood for ice-cream. Pistachio, hazelnut or coconut?"

"Sorry, I'm not in the mood for that either."

Rachel furrowed her brow.

"Then the situation is worse than I had thought."

"Why didn't my parents tell me, Rachel? If they kept from me something that big, what else might they have lied about?"

Her friend nodded and squeezed her hand.

"You have every right to feel betrayed, but remember, your parents probably did it because they worried about losing you."

"They wouldn't have lost me! I would have loved them just as much."

"But they couldn't know how you would react. Look at it from their point of view. Your birth mother clearly knew their home address. Possibly, they imagined her turning up to take you back and you choosing to go with her."

Alice sighed.

"But now I'm angry with them and with myself for being cross with them. I can't even ask them any questions now that they're..."

She couldn't say the word.

"No wonder I don't look anything like my parents. I have the genes of a stranger! From another country, too. What if there's a genetic disease in my birth parents' families? Don't some Mediterranean people have a genetic predisposition to sickle-cell anaemia?"

Rachel gave her a long hug then put an ice-cream tub on her lap.

"As you have at least fifty per cent Italian blood, you qualify for a complimentary tub of ice cream."

She put a spoon in Alice's hand.

"Try to look at the positives. Maybe you can apply for an Italian passport. And you probably have a birth mother still alive plus lots of blood relatives in

Italy."

Alice smiled weakly. It was all too shocking, too quick, too much.

If only she had never found those papers. She'd love to put them back into the chest in the loft and forget about them.

Instead, she was grieving her parents all over again.

"My birth mother called me Francesca," she mused.

"Are you going to look for her?"

"Yes," Alice answered without hesitation.

This wasn't a choice to make. She could not carry on with her life as if nothing had happened.

"And are you prepared for the possibility that she might not want to meet you?" Rachel warned.

"She wants to meet me, Rachel. Her letters make that very clear."

"Yes, but those letters are more than twenty years old. She might have moved on with her life and decided to put her past behind her."

"It's a risk I have to take."

Rachel hesitated.

"Another possibility is that you won't find her alive. Are you ready for that, too?"

"Yes, I am."

"Then that's all settled. And now we're going to dig into this ice-cream before it melts!"

That afternoon, Alice rang the phone number her birth mother had provided in her letters. It was a landline, of course, and she didn't hold much hope that Simona would still live there, but perhaps whoever lived there now would know of her.

Nobody answered; the line had been disconnected.

Alice wrote to the address she'd found in the letters and waited for a reply but the only one she got was her own letter, returned marked "addressee not known".

The letters she'd found in the loft hadn't borne Simona's surname so an internet search was impossible.

Alice turned to the Italian adoption tribunal for help but was informed they couldn't release her birth mother's details because she had never authorised the disclosure.

Her frustration mounted just as her curiosity and her conjectures grew.

In what predicament had her birth mother found herself to give away her baby?

CHAPTER 4

"Hi chum. Tell me, how is your search going?" Rachel asked Alice over the phone one day.

"I've hit a wall," she confessed. "I can't think of anything else I can do except go to Calabria myself and search on the ground, starting from the address that was in the letters."

"It might be a trip for nothing," her friend warned.

"I know but it's my only option."

"I understand. When are you thinking of going?"

"Next week. I know that until I've found my birth mother I won't be able to think of anything else, so I'd better do this as soon as possible."

Rachel hesitated. "I'd love to come with you, Alice, but I can't leave work at the moment."

"No worries. I'll go on my own," she replied.

"What? You shouldn't go on your own."

"Rach, I'm twenty-seven."

"I know that, but do you speak any Italian?"

"Well, no."

"Okay, let's think about this. Isn't there a cute Italian waiter working with you at the hotel?"

Alice smiled. She had never told Rachel that Paolo was cute, so her friend must have met him when she had visited her at work.

True, with his warm brown eyes and infectious smile, Paolo was a very attractive man.

He didn't work at the hotel

anymore, however.

"He left two months ago."

"You've got his number, I hope."

"Yes, when I was organising his leaving do. He will find it a bit weird if I call him out of the blue, though!"

"You're going to have to do much weirder things if you want to find your birth mother in a foreign country!"

Rachel was right. Alice had no idea how she was to look for a woman she knew nothing about except her first name.

"Ask him to come with you and be your interpreter. If you're going to deal with Italian bureaucracy, you'll definitely need help from a local," Rachel advised.

It made sense.

"Fine. I'll call him."

CHAPTER 5

Paolo had pulled his suitcase out from under the bed and was shaking the dust off when his phone rang. He shuddered, again thinking that it might be Gus chasing him about the sketches, but it was Alice Baker, the receptionist of the hotel where he had worked previously.

She had been a nice girl and they might have become good friends if he had stayed longer there, but the hours hadn't been compatible with his lessons at the Academy.

What could she be ringing about?

"Hi, Alice. What a nice surprise," he

said cautiously.

"Am I disturbing you?" She sounded shy.

"Not at all. How are you?"

"Well, thanks. And you?"

"I'm well, too."

One of the first things he had learnt on his arrival to the UK was that "How are you?" was a rhetorical question to which he wasn't expected to answer truthfully.

"Do I remember correctly that you come from Calabria?" she asked.

"Yes. Why?"

"I'm planning to visit there and, er, I think I need some help with the language."

"Okay, I know some good phone apps. You hover your phone's camera over a text and they translate it for you. I'll send you the names."

"Thanks, but I meant I want to communicate with the locals, have proper conversations. The thing is, I was wondering if you would be my interpreter, Paolo. I'm planning to visit the city of Reggio Calabria and perhaps the area around it."

"I see."

He had never been asked anything like this, but Reggio Calabria wasn't far from Altavicia and he liked the idea of travelling home with someone else.

He had left Italy in a cloud of anger and disillusionment. Those feelings might swamp him again as soon as he landed, but it was less likely with company and distraction.

"Actually, your request is well timed because I'm flying home in one week's time and my village isn't far from Reggio Calabria. So, yes, that would work. I could spend a couple of days with you."

"I might need you for more than a couple of days. Maybe one week. I would pay you, of course."

Could he spare a week? Yes. The

more reasons he had to be away from the family home and Marcello, the better.

He wouldn't take payment from Alice but maybe she could help him in return. She could stay with his family and divert their attention from him.

His family loved visitors, and a girl from England would be a major attraction. Everyone would be swarming around her and nobody would be studying him to work out whether he was over Rosaria and had forgiven his brother.

Even better, if Alice came to the wedding with him, he would be so busy translating for her and explaining about Italian weddings that he wouldn't have time to think about what his brother had done.

"I'll do it, but I don't want any money. Instead, I'd like you to come and stay with my family."

He decided not to mention the

wedding, in case it scared her off.

"That would be lovely! But why?"

"I hate all the attention I get when I go home. My family love visitors so you would be a distraction for them."

"Great! It'll be wonderful to meet a real Italian family."

They discussed flights then closed the call.

CHAPTER 6

"Mamma, I'm bringing a friend with me. She'll stay with us, if that's okay."

For a few seconds, it looked like his mother's picture on his phone's screen had frozen. Then Lia's smile turned into a grin.

"Why didn't you tell me that you've got a new sweetheart?"

"Alice is just a friend."

How could his mum think that he would embark into a romantic relationship after devoting ten years of his life to Rosaria?

He had put aside his dreams of studying at the Royal Academy of Arts in London because she hadn't wanted to move to the UK, and in the end she had dumped him for his brother, leaving his heart in smithereens.

He would be mad to put himself through that again. Now that he was thirty, it was time to put himself and his dreams first.

He would never entrust his heart and his future to the hands of a woman who could then toss it away.

His mother chuckled.

"I don't mind what you call each other. In my days, we had sweethearts, fiancées, husbands and wives. Nowadays, there are so many new words that I can't keep up."

"Like I say, Alice is a friend."

"I hope things are going to be fine between you and your brother now."

Ah, this was the crux of the matter. His mother wanted him to have a new girlfriend because she thought that, through that, he would forget Rosaria and forgive Marcello.

She was wrong. Paolo had long stopped having feelings for Rosaria but it hadn't helped him forgive her or his brother. Maybe he never would.

"It makes a mother's heart cry to see her sons angry with each other."

His mother looked so sad that Paolo's chest tightened.

"I'm sorry you had to witness it."

There had been raised voices and terrible words between him and his brother before Paolo had exiled himself to London.

"You're happy now and that's all that matters. Is she English or Italian? Blonde or brunette? Did you say her name is 'Alees'?"

He wanted to insist that he and Alice *really* were just friends, but he didn't have the heart to wipe the happy smile off his mother's face.

Could he and Alice pretend they were boyfriend and girlfriend, just for this holiday? From what he remembered about their time working together, she was an easy-going girl, happy to help others.

Perhaps she wouldn't mind helping him make his mum happy, especially as he was to be her interpreter in exchange.

"She's English and blonde."

"Like Princess Diana?"

"No."

"Well, so long as she's nice and kind and is good to you. What's her favourite Italian food? I'll cook that for our dinner."

Being allowed to choose the menu for a family meal was a privilege which was only bestowed on one's birthday.

"I don't know," he confessed.

"How can you not know? Don't you take her out for meals?"

"I haven't got the money, Mamma."

That was true. Until he got Gus's cheque, he was skint.

STEFANIA HARTLEY

"In fact, I'm sorry, but I'll have to work while I'm there. You won't see me very much."

"If you haven't got money then you should invite her to dinner in your home and cook for her."

His mother seemed more upset by the fact he hadn't invited Alice to dinner than the prospect of seeing little of him during his time at home. His distraction strategy was already working!

"Will Alees be helping you in your work? Is she an artist, too?"

"No, she's not. She'll be doing some sightseeing."

"Oh, good, then your sisters and I will look after her. We won't leave her for a moment alone," his mother said, beaming.

Uh, oh, this was not what he had expected.

"Alice will be fine on her own, Mamma. I've promised to take her to

31

Reggio Calabria for a few days," he explained, remembering his part of the deal.

"Quite right, too. Still, whenever you're busy doing your work, we will be with her. Don't worry, leave it to me."

The prospect of his mother and sisters let loose on Alice without him was terrifying rather than reassuring. Nevertheless, Paolo knew his mother well enough to understand that he wasn't going to be able to dissuade her over the phone.

"Thank you, Mamma."

He would sort the problem out when they were face to face.

Something else would have to wait for a face-to-face conversation, too—asking Alice to play along with the boyfriend/girlfriend charade.

CHAPTER 7

It was only after their plane was up in the sky and there was no way to get off that Paolo felt it safe to broach the girlfriend matter with Alice.

She was leaning her head against the headrest with her eyes closed, the picture of serenity. He let his gaze linger on her features. She was quite pretty. He cleared his voice.

"Alice, there's something I need to ask you. A favour."

She opened her eyes, sat up and smiled.

"Sure. Tell me."

Some   people   recoiled   at   the

word "favour", so her reaction was encouraging.

"When I told my mamma that you were coming and staying with us, there was a little misunderstanding."

"Oh, Paolo, you mustn't worry! I can stay in a hotel. It's no problem at all. That was my original plan anyway."

"That's not the misunderstanding we had."

As she looked at him with her big innocent eyes full of kindness, he felt his courage drain away and guilt replace it. He shouldn't be springing this on her at 34,000 feet in the sky!

"What was this misunderstanding?" she pressed.

He took a deep breath.

"That you're my girlfriend."

"You told her that wasn't true, though?"

"I should have, but I didn't."

"Why not?"

"She was so happy."

STEFANIA HARTLEY

Alice frowned.

"Why? Have you never had a girlfriend?"

Paolo winced. He hated telling the story of Rosaria's betrayal. But the refreshment trolley was on its way and, if he didn't hurry, he would be telling his sorry story to the hostesses, too!

"I had one for ten years before she left me for my brother. I'm going home for their wedding," he said in one breath as if he was swallowing a bitter medicine.

Her eyes widened and her mouth turned into an 'o'. He braced himself for the words of pity that usually followed the shock each time he told his story. Instead, she waited for him to continue.

"Mamma thinks that I'll be broken-hearted until I find love again."

"Are you still broken-hearted?" Alice asked.

"Any drinks or snacks?" the hostess asked cheerfully.

"No, thanks." Paolo turned to Alice. "I'm not broken-hearted at all. I'm just angry with them for going behind my back. They had been in love with each other for a long time before they were brave enough to tell me. All that time I was giving up my dream of going to London to study because I knew that Rosaria would never leave Altavicia. I wasted years planning a future in Altavicia with Rosaria while she dreamed of a future with my brother instead."

"So, your mother wants to see you with another woman because she hopes that, then, you will forgive your brother?"

"Correct."

"If you want to reassure your mum, then why not find a real girlfriend? A guy like you..."

Paolo noticed the hint of a blush

on her cheeks. Was she paying him a compliment?

"I'm done with relationships," he said. "From now on, it's going to be just me and my art."

She narrowed her eyes.

"Let me understand this. You asked me to come and stay with your family so that you can trick your mother?"

He shook his head vigorously.

"Not at all! I wouldn't have considered passing you off as my girlfriend if my mum hadn't misunderstood me when I told her about your visit."

"I really don't like to trick people, Paolo. After what your ex-girlfriend did to you, you shouldn't either."

"I don't," he pleaded. "I tried to tell my mother that she was mistaken, but she ignored my protests. Look, Alice, nothing will be expected of you. My parents are very strict about public displays of affection so you won't even have to hold my hand! All I'm asking of you is that you don't contradict me. You won't have to lie—my parents don't speak English and my siblings very little. Every communication will have to go through me."

She crossed her arms and lifted an eyebrow.

"In fact, you'll do all the lying!"

"I won't lie, I just won't tell them the truth. Apart from the wedding and the odd meal, we won't be with my family anyway. Most of the time, we'll be exploring Reggio Calabria as you wished."

These last words dissipated Alice's frown a little and she sighed.

"Okay."

CHAPTER 8

For the rest of the journey, Alice mulled over the girlfriend ruse. Was it right to deceive someone if that deception, far from hurting them, was sure to make them happy?

She was still on the fence about that but definitely wasn't pleased about Paolo springing it on her on the plane.

Then again, she conceded, she hadn't told Paolo the real reason for her own trip yet. As far as he was aware, she was just sightseeing.

Indignation and guilt swirled inside her, but her bad mood evaporated when the automatic doors of Reggio

Calabria's airport opened into the arrivals hall and a cacophony of excitement and happiness swamped her.

People were shouting, laughing, calling each other from a distance, waving and smiling.

This was Italy and she was going to be a part of it. By blood, she already was!

"There they are."

Paolo pointed with his chin and waved back to a tubby woman who was waving with both arms at them.

She pushed her way through the crowd and managed to reach them before they had even cleared the exit.

His mother swept Paolo into an embrace, then pulled back to look at him and touch his cheeks, as if to make sure that it was really him and not a ghost.

"*Ciao, Mamma.*"

He bent down and gave her a kiss on

each cheek, looking at her tenderly.

Was this the way Italians loved each other?

She gazed at him with an ecstatic grin, pinching his cheeks affectionately and blabbering away in Italian, oblivious to other travellers who had to manoeuvre their suitcases around them awkwardly.

She had Paolo's eyes, Alice saw —warm and kind with a hint of mischievousness. Also, his impossibly long eyelashes.

His mother turned to Alice and said something in Italian before pulling her into an embrace so tight that Alice could feel against her chest the brooch pinned on the other woman's shoulder.

She was warm, soft and smelled of basil and tomatoes. Alice's heart gave a somersault. How would it be if her birth mother was like this woman and welcomed her in the same way?

Lia pulled away to study Alice's face,

taking her all in.

"Bellissima ragazza!"

Beautiful girl? She wasn't beautiful, she knew. This must be an Italian figure of speech.

A man who looked like an older version of Paolo joined them. He hugged Paolo, kissed him on both cheeks, then hugged her too, explaining that his name was Agostino.

Paolo's mother was bouncing around Paolo in a high state of excitement, speaking in rapid-fire Italian with a huge grin on her face.

Alice could see why he hadn't had the heart to disappoint her.

Meanwhile, Agostino was trying to steer his wife towards the exit, waving a parking ticket in the air and protesting, perhaps about the parking times.

Even in the midst of this ebullient welcome, Paolo's family wasn't the most chaotic one there. The arrivals hall was ringing with excited voices.

When they finally started walking to the exit, Paolo dropped back with Alice.

"Everything okay?" he whispered into her ear, giving her goosebumps.

"Yes, thank you."

When they got to the car, it became clear almost immediately that there wasn't enough space in the boot for all their luggage.

"I'm sorry, I overpacked," Alice said.

She always did that when she was uncertain about what she would find at the other end of her journey. This trip certainly was rife with uncertainties.

"It's fine. There's more space than it seems," Paolo answered, shifting the suitcases around in the boot.

Alice was staring at his toned biceps when a roughened hand wrapped around hers and pulled her firmly towards the car's back seat.

It was Paolo's mother, opening the rear door for her and inviting her in.

Alice wriggled into the car and the older woman sat in the seat next to her with a grin, without releasing her hand.

Paolo's father was sitting in the front passenger seat while Paolo took the driver's seat.

Alice reached for the seatbelt but couldn't find it at first. It was buried behind the seat. Clearly it hadn't been used often.

Paolo's mother said something to her, waving her hand in the air.

"What is your mum saying?" Alice asked Paolo.

"She says that you don't need a seatbelt because I'm a very good driver," he answered with an impish grin.

Suddenly it dawned on Alice how totally she would have to rely on

Paolo for every communication with his family.

She smiled at his mum and, pretending not to have understood, dug her hand into the crack between the seats, pulled out her seatbelt and buckled up.

She was glad she had because, as soon as they pulled out of the car park, it seemed that Italy had a different highway code than the UK—if it had any at all!

It wasn't simply a matter of cars keeping to the right instead of the left or coming from the other side at roundabouts. Worse was the feeling that the roads could be compared to the dance floor of a nightclub. Cars seemed to be allowed to take any available space, wherever it was found. Occasionally, they were even permitted to touch each other so long as it was done gently.

At several points in the journey,

Alice had to stifle a gasp. Paolo was a good driver, she could see, but that wasn't the case for some of the other motorists.

Slow vehicles straddled the breakdown lane, pieces of furniture were transported in open car boots held down with string, and speeding cars bombed down the slow lane, shamelessly undertaking.

All this took place accompanied by a sprinkling of motorbikes which threaded their way between the cars with unpredictable trajectories.

Alice tried her best to keep her horror from showing on her face. She thought she succeeded because, every now and then, Paolo's mother would glance at her with a happy grin and pat her knee.

Tenderness and guilt marbled Alice's feelings. All this love with which she was being showered with was based on a falsehood. This woman loved her because she thought she was Paolo's girlfriend. Instead, she was no more than a fraud.

Eventually, Paolo would have to tell his mother the truth or make up a story that he and Alice had broken up. Either way, the poor woman was going to be upset. Then surely Paolo would regret the ruse.

Alice was already regretting it.

CHAPTER 9

The whitewashed house was surrounded by a beautiful little garden enclosed by a rough-plastered wall. A squat fig tree with dark green leaves and little pear-shaped fruits took pride of place in the middle of the flowerbed, surrounded by hibiscuses in vibrant red. A pink bougainvillea cascaded over the wall while geraniums flanked the drive with an explosion of Ferrari-red flowers.

Alice stroked the fig's furry leaves which had been warmed by the sun. The air smelled of flowers, freshly baked bread, rosemary and meat.

"Your family lives in the garden of Eden!" she said to Paolo.

"I think we've passed that stage. We're in the Cain and Abel part of the story now."

The bitterness in his voice told her he was thinking of Rosaria and Marcello and she felt sorry for him.

His parents had disappeared inside when two girls, one in her late teens or early twenties and the other much younger, shot out the front door.

The older one was willowy and dark. Clever make-up enhanced her remarkable eyes and lips. Alice had often wondered how other women managed to perfect that feline flick of eyeliner.

The younger one was chubby and bouncy. Alice placed her at around twelve years old.

They came over to Alice with open arms and hugged and kissed her on both cheeks.

"Hello! We've heard a lot about you," they informed her in English.

Alice shot Paolo a glance. He had assured her nobody would be talking to her in English so she would not have to tell fibs.

She would normally have said that she had heard a lot about them, but it was not true. She and Paolo weren't even in the second hour of their fake relationship and she was already struggling to keep up the pretence!

"I hope good things," she replied cautiously, hoping for some information. What could he have told them when he knew so little about her?

Paolo said something to his sisters in Italian which Alice guessed meant something like "Leave her alone", then took her hand and led her through a tiled path that circled the house and to the back garden.

"You told me no-one spoke English

but you!" she whispered once they were alone.

"I didn't think my sisters paid attention in their English classes at school."

"This ruse isn't going to work, Paolo! They're going to suss us out. How can I be your girlfriend if I don't know anything about your family?"

"There's not much to know. My youngest sister is Agatina. She's sweet and nice when she tries and when she's not with my other sister, Vittoria. She's a bit of trouble, that one, but nothing to worry about." He spoke flippantly but the tension in his jaw told her that he was unsure as well.

They emerged onto a patio at the back of the house where a table laid for perhaps 20 stretched under a pergola and beyond. The place was teeming with people.

"Oh, my!" This was no intimate family supper. It looked more like a celebration. "You didn't tell me your brother's wedding celebrations started now!"

"I didn't know." He sighed.

This was overwhelming. She needed time alone to think what to do. "I need the toilet."

"I'll take you."

He led her into the house by a backdoor and down a corridor to a downstairs toilet.

"Shall I wait?"

"No, I can find my way back. You go and talk to your family, answer all their questions so that they won't ask me, because I won't be able to answer."

"Understood."

She locked the door, leaned against it and took a couple of deep breaths. The small room made her feel safe and contained.

The place was spotless. A linen towel hung on the towel rail, still with its ironing creases. *Buongiorno* was embroidered in delicate pink thread, and silky tassels hung at the bottom. It was such a pretty thing that Alice was loth to dry her hands on it. What if it was only for decoration? Instead, she tore off some toilet roll and used that.

A splash of cold water on her face restored her and she felt ready to face the challenges of the evening ahead.

When she came out of the room, however, it was to find a young woman in front of the door. A shock of curly hair framed her delicate face and beautiful green eyes.

"I'm sorry," Alice said.

"Hello! You must be Alice. Lovely to meet you," the other woman said, offering her hand and smiling.

CHAPTER 10

There were cut flowers on the dresser in the corridor. As Rosaria was allergic to pollen, these flowers couldn't be for the wedding couple but for Alice. His mother had really gone out of her way to honour his presumed girlfriend.

He shouldn't have let her believe that Alice was his girlfriend but should have burst his mum's bubble as soon as it had started.

For one thing, it wasn't fair on Alice. He had hoped she would take the focus of attention from him but not in this way.

All the things he had promised

her—no fibs, no questions, no interrogations—were turning out impossible to keep.

He surveyed the crowd of family and friends chatting, laughing and milling around between the flowerbeds, trellises and pergolas.

Now they had to face this family gathering. Alice was going to hate it.

One thought gave him a surge of panic. Was this a welcome party for Alice?

Surely not. His mother wouldn't have sprung it on him without warning and certainly wouldn't have invited all these people. He and Alice weren't even supposed to be engaged.

No, this had to be a pre-wedding party for Marcello and Rosaria.

From the crowd of family and friends Rosaria appeared and walked over to him. Paolo tensed, ready for the feelings of hurt that had accompanied her presence ever since

THE ITALIAN FAKE DATE

the debacle. But fear was larger than hurt.

"Hi, Paolo," she began tentatively.

"Hi."

"Thank you for coming."

He nodded. He wasn't going to tell her that his mother had strong-armed him with emotional blackmail.

"It means a lot to Marcello and me. And congratulations about your girlfriend. I've just spoken to her and she seems really nice," Rosaria continued.

"You've spoken to Alice?"

"Yes. We met outside the toilet just now." She smiled a little sheepishly, "I've started English language lessons."

"I thought you hated English."

"I only hated it because I didn't like the idea of living in England."

He didn't like the reference to their past. "I'd better go and find Alice." It was as much out of concern for Alice as a wish to stop this conversation.

"Of course," Rosaria said.

Paolo walked off and scanned the crowd, looking for Alice. He found her surrounded by his younger cousins. He walked over to her with the intention of shooing people away from her but, just then, his mother called everyone to the table. Perfect timing.

He made sure to sit next to Alice so that he could shield her from any prying questions.

His father raised a bottle of bubbly and, shouting over all the other excited voices, ordered everyone to take a plastic cup to join in with a toast. Paolo didn't feel like toasting Marcello and Rosaria, but if he didn't, his parents would notice and be sad.

Marcello was sitting at the opposite end of the table. Like Paolo he, too, had done his best to avoid a meeting.

"Let's toast the happy couple!" their father bellowed and popped the corks of one, two and three bottles of bubbly. Everyone clapped. Reluctantly, Paolo picked up his cup and filled it.

He looked in his brother's direction, ready for the toast, only to find that Marcello, Rosaria and everyone else were looking at him instead.

"To Paolo and Alice"— his father bellowed, raising his plastic cup —"with all our wishes and hopes that Paolo gets his act together and doesn't let this one slip away!"

"Let this one slip away"? Was his father actually blaming him for Rosaria switching to his brother? Paolo's blood roiled. Everyone cheered.

"Translate for Alice!" his father demanded but his voice was drowned by a chorus initiated by Paolo's younger sisters.

"*Bacio*! Kiss!"

Paolo could have strangled every

member of his family.

"Not now," he protested but the chanting continued.

"*Bacio!*"

He glanced at Alice. Her flaming cheeks told him that she didn't need a translator to understand what they were asking. He wanted to mouth a silent apology to her but everyone was watching. There was no way out.

She looked into his eyes and nodded. He bent down, she met him halfway and they brushed a gentle kiss on each other's lips.

It was the softest kiss he had ever given or received.

CHAPTER 11

Alice opened her eyes and landed gently back on earth. How could such a soft kiss spin her like a hurricane? The whole evening had rocked her. Paolo's family and friends had lavished her with such affection and attention. She wasn't used to it.

Paolo, too, was being showered with love. So many people looked genuinely happy to see him. Some brave souls had tried to express their approval of her choice in broken English or with winks and thumbs-up.

The one who had most surprised her was Paolo's ex-girlfriend. Rosaria had introduced herself and told her what a thoroughly nice, trustworthy and devoted man he was.

"Clearly not good enough for you, though," Alice had managed not to retort.

She had seen the hurt in Paolo's eyes when he told her about Rosaria's betrayal, and couldn't help holding it against this woman.

She could believe what Rosaria was telling her about him. Wasn't the fact that Paolo had travelled back for the wedding, proof that he was forgiving and generous?

The lengths he was prepared to go to, also, to make his mum happy—like pretending he had a girlfriend.

Alice had better not forget that their relationship wasn't real. He wasn't in love with her, and his family had welcomed her only because they thought that she was special to him.

That wasn't true, though the

memory of the kiss lingered on her lips.

The rest of the meal went smoothly.

"After dinner, we're going to a concert and you're coming, too!" the youngest of Paolo's sisters told her excitedly.

"A famous tenor who grew up in Altavicia is giving a free concert in the town square," Paolo explained. "Luigi Felice"

Alice didn't disclose that she had never heard of the man, didn't listen to classical music and couldn't stand opera.

This would be an interesting experience. Embracing her Italian origins required being open to new things.

***

A temporary stage had been erected at one end of the town square and decorative lights were strewn between the buildings. Spotlights created a beautiful effect on the façade of the baroque church which provided a stunning background to the show.

When the tenor climbed onto the stage the crowd cheered, whistled and clapped enthusiastically. He addressed them to the sound of more cheering and applause. He was clearly the town's hero.

When he started singing, Alice understood why. His throat must be made of velvet, silver and molten chocolate!

Alice closed her eyes to taste and touch the sound. This music, composed centuries ago, transported her to another time. It was surreal and she was loving it.

"I'm sorry about everything that's happened tonight. I hadn't meant it to go this way," Paolo whispered in her ear.

She opened her eyes, embarrassed to have been caught in a moment of abandonment.

What was he sorry about? The family dinner that had turned into an engagement party? Or the kiss?

She could never tell him that she hadn't minded the kiss at all nor that part of her wished there could be more.

"You love your mum and you wanted to make her happy," she replied.

"I'm glad you understand."

"I do."

"Are you close to your mother?"

Alice should have seen this question coming. Now was the time to come clean about the real reason for her trip.

"It depends which mother you mean. The one that brought me up, yes, I was close to—at least, I thought I was. The one who gave birth to me I've never met her. This is why I'm doing this trip: I want to find her."

She waited for his reaction but he

was silent. Only the tenor's notes fluttered on the warm night air.

"I need your help," she continued. "I should have told you earlier."

"Yes, you should have," he said.

"I'm sorry. I was afraid, just as you were when you didn't tell me about the fake-girlfriend business until I was already on the plane."

"Touché," he conceded.

"Paolo, the bottom line is that I'm helping you make your mother happy and you can help me find mine."

Her words sounded a bit like "an eye for an eye" which wasn't what Alice had meant. The tenor held a note for what felt like an interminable time. "What do you say?"

CHAPTER 12

What Alice had just said made sense. Paolo owed her. He could hardly take the moral high ground because he had done to her just what she was doing to him now.

There was a difference, however.

"Faking a relationship doesn't hurt anyone. What you're planning may hurt many people."

"I don't see how!" she protested.

"Uncovering secrets from the past is bound to cause hurt and upset. Alice, if your mother gave you away she must have had her reasons. Perhaps she didn't want anyone to know that she was pregnant. What will happen if you turn up on her doorstep? You could wreck families."

The tenor finished his last note and the audience burst into a long applause.

Alice bit her bottom lip.

"It's important that I find my birth mother. She was looking for me, you see. My parents didn't reply to her letters."

"This isn't Britain, it is southern Italy. Pregnancy outside wedlock is still frowned upon and would have been even more so at the time when your birth mother had you."

Alice sighed in frustration. "I'm not going to ignore her letters just in case she's embarrassed by me! When you asked me to pose as your girlfriend you promised that all I had to do was not to contradict you. Instead, I was told to kiss you in front of all your family. Surely, asking for your help with some translation and interpreting is reasonable," she said.

"That's not the point. I disagree with what you're trying to do. I cannot help you because what you're doing is wrong."

He had tried to keep his voice down but Vittoria turned around and glanced at them.

Alice scowled at him. "Then our exchange is off. Tomorrow morning I'll leave your parents' place and begin my search on my own. You can tell your parents we've broken up; that it was a fraud or a mistake or a misunderstanding. Whatever you want."

The first notes of the aria "*La Donna è Mobile*" from "Rigoletto" started.

Paolo clenched his fists. He needed silence and peace to think and the rumbustious melody was adding to his irritation.

The lyrics—women are fickle like

feathers in the wind—reminded him of the truth he had learned with Rosaria.

He should never have entered into this crazy agreement with Alice and it was probably a good thing they were stopping now before it went too far.

It might already have gone too far for him. He had introduced Alice to his family who had loved her at first sight. They were going to feel sad, even guilty, if she broke up with him immediately after meeting them!

He would be sad, too. They had only spent a day together but he had grown attached to her. As a friend, he reminded himself, banishing the memory of that kiss.

Vittoria leaned over. "Mamma wants me to buy sweets at the stall for everyone. What would you two like?" she asked in English.

"I'm fine, thanks," Alice replied.

"My mamma will not accept 'no' for an answer," Paolo told her. "If you don't say what you want, Vittoria will buy one of everything and you'll have to try them all."

"Then I guess I'd better go with your sister and choose something. Damage limitation," she added with a wry smile.

Paolo watched his sister and Alice walk over to the street stalls and thought about Alice's phrase. *Damage limitation.*

Whether he helped her or not, Alice was going to look for her birth mother. If he agreed to help her, perhaps, he could limit the damage. Not getting involved was the worst thing he could do.

Alice and Vittoria returned with several small bags of sweets and Alice offered him one.

"This is not a peace offering. It's only for your sister's eyes," she murmured under her breath with a saccharine smile.

He took the bag. "I am going to help you find your mother."

"Oh, the marvels a bag of sweets can do!" she exclaimed, mocking,

He smiled.

"Tell me the truth: what made you change your mind?"

Just then, the tenor completed his aria on the inconstancy of women to another roar of applause.

"Blame it on the inconstancy of men," he told her and shrugged.

CHAPTER 13

They were sitting at the ceramic tiled table under the pergola, dipping breakfast biscuits into their cups of caffellatte cups, planning the day ahead.

Alice showed Paolo the address she had copied from Simona's letters. He sighed.

"Reggio Calabria is a city, not a village. Here in Altavicia people die in the same houses they were born and lived all their life. In Reggio it's not the same. There's a good chance that your birth mother has moved from there."

"I understand but this address is all I

have to go on. How far is it?"

"Forty-five minutes on the Vespa."

"I don't ride motorbikes," she warned.

"You won't have to ride it at all. You'll just sit on it."

Alice tried to steady her nerves. She used to love being on her father's big touring motorbike but since her parents had lost their lives she couldn't look at a motorbike without thinking about their accident. "I don't ride pillion either."

"Seriously? Riding a Vespa is the most pleasurable thing I can think of."

"I'm sorry, I can't."

"May I ask why?"

She didn't want to tell him about her parents' accident. It was pathetic to be so afraid. Motorbikes hadn't suddenly become more dangerous just because her parents had been unlucky on one rainy day.

There was no rain in Calabria in this

season and Paolo surely thought her very silly.

"I don't trust Italian road users, motorbike riders least of all," she excused herself.

"I'm a very safe rider. You won't have to do anything other than hold on tight and lean in with me."

She didn't know which was scarier, the fact that she needed to hold on tight or the thought of leaning over the road.

He shook his head. "As you wish. We'll take the car. Then our revised travel time is a little over one hour."

"What are you going to do in Reggio?" Vittoria asked in English, coming out of the house and joining them at the table.

"Hi, Vittoria." Alice liked Paolo's sister and enjoyed having someone else to talk to directly, without translation.

"Really, there's no privacy in this

house," Paolo protested.

Vittoria smiled at Alice and frowned at her brother. "If there's no privacy here blame it on Mamma. I tried to persuade her to give you two a room together but she wouldn't have it."

Vittoria pulled out a chair next to Alice and sat down. "Why are you going to Reggio?" she asked again. "There's nothing there."

"How about the Riace bronzes?" Paolo countered.

"That's something to look at in the winter. Right now it's time for being beside the sea. You can't beat it, Alice."

"Thanks, we'll think about it," Paolo replied, draining his caffellatte. "Ready when you are," he told Alice.

***

The road from Altavicia to Reggio Calabria went through villages and small towns but in the gaps between the houses Alice caught glimpses of the sea. It was a kaleidoscope of turquoise, cobalt and specks of gold.

"I thought eucalyptus trees only grew in Australia," she said, noticing the mottled bark of the trees on the sides of the road.

"The climate is quite arid here, too," he explained.

"What's that pillar of smoke? Look!" She pointed to a stretch of land on the other side of the sea. "Actually, no, don't look. Keep your eyes on the road."

"I don't need to look. That's Etna."

"The volcano! Isn't it in Sicily?"

"Sicily in just on the other side of the waters."

Now Alice had something else to worry about on top of the road traffic: an active volcano billowing smoke! "Is it erupting at the moment?"

"Only a little; nothing to worry about. Our volcanologists keep a constant watch on it."

"If you say so."

"You have a lot of worries. You won't enjoy your Italian holiday and experience *la dolce vita* if you don't let go of them."

"I'm not here to enjoy myself," she reminded him.

"Ah, yes, I forgot."

Paolo seemed to be driving more slowly than on the journey back from the airport. Was he trying to prove to her that she could trust him on the road?

If he was trying to help her relax, it didn't work as they were soon stuck in a traffic jam with mopeds and scooters slaloming between the stationary cars, increasing her stress levels.

At one red traffic light they found themselves behind a bride's car.

"Oh, dear, I hope she's not going to be late!" Alice said.

"Nobody will mind. It's custom for brides to be late, though some of them take it to ridiculous levels."

"Are you ready for your brother's wedding?" she asked.

"If you mean have I got something to wear, yes. I haven't bought them a present, yet. Perhaps I'll get them a set of knives."

His tone left her unsure whether he was serious about the knives or was jesting.

"Sorry, you probably don't want to talk about your brother's wedding."

"I'm fine about it. I think you might find interesting how different Italian weddings are from British ones."

"Tell me."

"For one thing, there are no best men or bridesmaids. We only have witnesses, one for the bride and one for the groom. In a church wedding you can have more than two, though."

"What do they do?"

"Their main job is to attend the ceremony and sign the official register of weddings to make the wedding legally valid. They have to be over eighteen and Italian citizens."

"Who is going to keep the bridegroom's and the bride's nerves in check, help with the preparations, provide the rings and so on?" she wanted to know.

"The witnesses can do all that, if they wish. It's an honour to be asked to be a wedding witness."

From the tone of his voice Alice guessed that his brother hadn't asked him. That was understandable, given the circumstances, but sad all the same.

"I guess that the first requisite of a wedding witness is to be able to attend the ceremony," she mused. "The second would be that they live close enough to the bride and groom to be able to help them with the preparations."

This was avoiding the main reason why his brother could not have asked him.

"Yes," Paolo agreed. "My brother has chosen our cousins and Rosaria her brother and sister. They all live in Altavicia."

Alice tried to imagine what it might be like to live surrounded by family in the same village. It might be stifling, but what a lot of support! Nobody would ever be alone, or have to clear their late parents' loft by themselves.

"You'll find out all about Italian weddings in a few days' time."

"What do you mean?"

"Marcello's wedding."

"Am I coming?"

"You're my girlfriend, remember?"

Of course. Being his girlfriend meant that she would be expected to attend family functions.

"I haven't got anything to wear."

"Italian weddings are a little less formal than British ones." He scanned her. She was wearing jeans and a T-shirt.

"I'm not going to wear jeans at a wedding!" she argued.

He smiled. "I wasn't going to suggest that. I was going to suggest you borrow something from Vittoria."

So when he had stared at her he hadn't been checking what she was wearing but her size. A frisson of embarrassment or excitement—she was unsure which—ran up her back.

CHAPTER 14

The satnav had taken them to a lungomare, a seafront road, lined with detached family homes.

"In English we say that a man's home is his castle but it looks like it's the Italians who have the best fortifications in their homes," Alice remarked, surveying the high metal fences and gates.

"We're a little more obsessed with security in Italy, especially in cities. Here is number seventy-five." Paolo stopped the car in front of a property with a spiky metal fence backed with metal sheeting. Nothing was there for curious eyes to see. "How are you planning to do this?" he asked.

"By ringing the bell," she said.

There was no need. As soon as they got out of the car they were welcomed by ferocious barking from behind the fence.

"That must be awful for the neighbours," Alice commented.

"They have dogs, too." Paolo pointed to a mastiff barking at the gate next door.

He checked the plaque on the intercom but there was no name. These people really cared about their privacy, which wasn't a good sign.

"Let's do this." Alice pressed the intercom's button.

A little later, a woman shouted from behind the gate. "What do you want?"

Paolo couldn't see her but he guessed from her tone that she wasn't friendly. He was already regretting this. He should have tried harder to talk Alice out of this hopeless mission.

"Ask her if she's Simona," Alice urged.

Paolo did so.

"No, she's not Simona and there is no Simona in her house," he relayed to Alice, leaving out the "go away" with which the woman had ended her reply.

Alice's quest might not be a hopeless one but the results could still turn out to be disappointing. He couldn't imagine Alice and this woman ever being friends with each other.

"Ask her if she knows anyone called Simona who lived here twenty-seven years ago."

Paolo asked the question.

"Why do you want to know?" the woman shouted back.

Did they really have to have this conversation through a metal screen over the din of barking dogs?

"We're long-lost family," he answered, without consulting Alice.

She would have probably told the woman the full story, which Paolo felt wasn't sensible.

"What's your surname?" the woman asked.

"Baker," Paolo answered, leaving himself out of it.

Thankfully, the dogs had switched from full-on barking to background growling and snarling.

"That's a foreign surname and you're not foreign. Show me a document," the woman insisted.

Paolo translated to Alice who pulled her passport from her bag and showed it to an eye peeping through a crack between the gate and its hinges.

"There have never been any foreign people in this house."

"The woman we're looking for is Italian," Paolo tried to explain without giving too much away.

There was silence for a moment, as the woman seemed to be considering.

"Next door is a holiday letting. There are foreigner people there every summer. If you want to contact the owner, the house is listed online."

She seemed slightly more helpful now that she had shifted their attention from her property to the one next door.

"That would make sense. My parents must have holidayed next door and that's how they would have met Simona!" Alice said, excitement lighting up her eyes.

"This still doesn't tell us where we can find her now," he argued, then turned to the woman. "Have you lived here long?"

"No," she said briefly. Now that they had returned to talking about her property, she was less forthcoming.

"Do you remember who lived here before you?" he begged.

"Filomena Caracciolo. She's the daughter of the butcher in Via della

Repubblica." The woman spoke easily, happy again to talk about others.

"Thank you."

That was a useful lead. They got back into the car and headed for Via della Repubblica.

The traffic was heavy and Paolo couldn't help looking at scooter riders with a pinch of envy. He realised, too, that Alice's refusal to trust his riding skills had piqued him a little.

When they finally got to the butcher's they found it shut, just like all the other shops on the street. In fact, now he thought about it, all the shops they'd passed in the entire city had been shut.

"Of course, it's Monday!" He slapped his forehead.

"What do you mean?"

"All shops in Italy are shut on Mondays."

"That's crazy," Alice said.

"No, that's normal."

"But it's absurd. It means that we can't make any more progress today."

"You must learn to be patient, Alice."

She sighed. "I guess this will stop me at least from hogging you for the rest of the day when you should spend some time with your family," she owned.

"I should."

He should also go up to his hut and search for inspiration. Thinking about Gus's commission gave him a pang of anxiety. This had never happened to him—to be at a creative standstill for so long.

Would he ever be able to move forward again?

CHAPTER 15

After having a shower, Alice had forgotten to bring her clean clothes into the bathroom with her. She wrapped the bath towel around her body and a hand towel around her hair, then crept out into the corridor intending to dash to her room without meeting anyone. Instead, she almost crashed into Marcello.

A corridor usually wide enough for two people, suddenly feels too narrow when one of them is wearing only a towel, Alice decided.

"Hi," she said, giving up on the option of pretending they hadn't seen each other.

They had been introduced on the first night but Alice had been so overwhelmed by everything—and, she must admit, a little prejudiced against the man—that she hadn't registered how much like Paolo he looked.

Marcello was slightly shorter and chunkier, with a pair of dazzling green eyes that matched Rosaria's, but the two brothers were substantially two versions of the same model.

"Hi," he replied with a warm smile.

Everyone was so nice to her because they thought that she was Paolo's girlfriend.

Just then, Paolo came out of his bedroom. His gaze darted from her to Marcello and his expression turned icy. She had never seen that look on him.

Marcello must have seen it, too, because he passed her quickly.

Had that been jealousy? But Paolo couldn't be jealous of her because she wasn't his real girlfriend.

She was about to dive into her bedroom to get dressed but noticed a bunch of keys in Paolo's hands and a satchel bag slung across his chest.

"Where are you off to?" she asked.

"To work. I'll be back at dinnertime or a little after."

"You work here as well?"

"Yes," he replied succinctly.

She wanted to know more. Was it a restaurant job like in London or something else? Was he helping out a friend, perhaps?

The encounter with Marcello had left some lingering coldness in his voice so she just said goodbye and went into her room.

He wasn't her real boyfriend and she had no right to know where he went, she reminded herself as she brushed her hair in front of the mirror.

When she'd finished and had got dressed, she went out on to the back terrace and found a deckchair in a shady spot where she could sit with a book.

Trumpet-shaped flowers dangled from the pergola, swaying like bells in the breeze. It was a lovely little corner and she was just about to start reading when Vittoria arrived with another deckchair which she opened next to Alice's.

"Do you mind the smell of nail varnish? I could paint your nails, too."

"The smell doesn't bother me and thanks, I'd love that." She had felt a little ungroomed since arriving in Italy.

Vittoria beamed.

"What colour would you like?"

She showed her a palette that ranged from pastel yellow to blood red, purple and black.

"I'll go for the yellow," Alice decided.

Vittoria nodded in approval. "It suits your skin tone."

Alice pondered this. She had always been darker than her parents. They had told her that one of the grandmothers was dark but, when Alice had asked to see a photo, they hadn't been able to produce one. Now she knew why.

In Reggio she had studied the women, looking for similarities with herself and even hoping to spot someone who looked like her and who might be Simona.

"Your look a lot like your brother," she told Vittoria to shift the focus away from herself.

"I guess that must be a compliment, given that you like him enough to be going out with him!" She lowered her voice. "We never thought Paolo would date again. He's told you what happened, hasn't he?"

"Yes." Alice hoped her knowledge wasn't going to be tested because, apart from the general gist of the situation, she knew very little.

"What is your opinion? I mean, of course you'd be glad that Rosaria left him. But, in principle, do you think Rosaria and Marcello wronged him?"

Alice considered.

"Paolo and Rosaria weren't married yet so I think that it was fair. When people date, they're just trying to see if they could be life partners. They are not yet committed. It would have been a completely different matter if they had been married. That would have been a no-no for me."

"That's what I think, too," Vittoria said, nodding. "Put your foot up and I'll paint your toenails."

"I thought you were doing yours first."

"No, I want to do yours before Paolo comes home, finds us together and takes you away. He's so jealous of you!"

"I don't think so." Alice chuckled inwardly. The reason Paolo was keeping her away from his family was to avoid their questions!

"It's true," Vittoria insisted. "Maybe it's because of what happened with Rosaria. He took it badly. In a way, I understand it because they had been going out for ages but I don't think he was really in love with her."

"What makes you say that?" Paolo seemed a thoughtful and caring guy. Alice couldn't imagine him being a neglectful boyfriend.

Vittoria put the nailbrush down and looked her in the eyes. "Because he's never looked at her the way he looks at you."

Alice blinked. The girl was clearly off the scent there.

"This is why I can't understand why he's still so bitter about Rosaria and Marcello," Vittoria went on.

"Perhaps there are several things at play here. Wounded pride, sibling rivalry and the regret for all the things he had given up for the sake of his relationship with Rosaria. Like moving to London to study." Alice regretted saying this immediately because she was hovering over the furthest limits of what she knew about Paolo. She had no idea what he had wanted to study in London. It could have been ballet for all she knew.

Vittoria was looking at her starry-eyed. "You're right, that's all true! I can see that you know him so well."

Alice kept a straight face.

"Tell me, how did you two meet?" Vittoria urged.

Oh, dear. She and Paolo should have agreed in advance an "origin story". All she could do now was try to stick as much as possible to the truth. "We met at work."

"He didn't tell me that."

Oops. "Really? What has he told you?" she asked with forced nonchalance.

"It doesn't matter because I don't believe what he said anyway. I don't see you as that kind of girl."

This didn't sound good. "Then most likely it isn't true."

Vittoria didn't look entirely convinced. "You didn't fight over him with another girl in a nightclub and give her a black eye?"

Alice snorted. "Not at all!"

They talked about nightclubs and music. Alice admitted that nightclubs weren't her favourite hangouts. Then it was time to help out in the kitchen for supper.

Lia and Agatina were already working away when Alice and Vittoria joined them but there were still jobs for everyone: shelling beans, washing vegetables and dressing salads.

Vittoria translated for Alice but even when she wasn't translating Lia didn't stop talking to Alice in Italian.

Each time Alice didn't understand,

Lia repeated her words at a slower speed. This left Alice to guess, often with results that left everyone in stitches.

Agatina asked her about her favourite dishes and volunteered hers in great detail. Alice got the impression that favourite dishes might be the current topic in Agatina's English classes.

Paolo's father enquired about the dinner menu and disappeared into the cellar to choose the right wine.

Judging by the time it took him to reappear, the choice must have required a lot of thought.

CHAPTER 16

Marcello didn't join them for dinner that night. Alice wondered whether it had to do with her being there on her own. It was clear that Paolo wasn't over the matter of Rosaria and his brother.

Would he ever be? Was it really just resentment and sibling rivalry or could he still be in love with Rosaria? If so, it would explain why he hadn't been dating another woman but had had to resort to producing Alice as a fake girlfriend. The thought left her sad.

All through the meal, she kept an ear out for the sound of Paolo's Vespa, but he didn't return. Where was he right now and what was his work? Did he enjoy it or did he do it out of necessity? Crucially, even if she couldn't admit it to herself, did he enjoy it more than spending time with her?

After dinner, she swallowed her pride and turned to Vittoria. "Where does Paolo work?"

"In his hut."

The answer raised more questions, like what he was doing in a hut. Still, Alice admitting that she didn't know the location of his work was one thing. Revealing that she didn't have a clue what work he did, was another!

"Where is this hut?"

"Hasn't he shown you?"

"No."

"I don't know exactly where it is —I've never been—but it's somewhere up in the mountains." Vittoria pointed towards the dark shapes silhouetted against the starry sky. "He is very secretive about it. I guess he doesn't want anyone to disturb him while he's creating."

"Creating what?" Alice blurted out before reflecting that, as a girlfriend, she certainly should know.

If this blunder wasn't going to make Vittoria suspicious about their relationship, she didn't know what would!

Irritation pricked her. Paolo shouldn't have put her in this situation.

"He hasn't told you?" Vittoria asked.

"He's a very private person," Alice replied feebly.

"Well, as far as I know, he makes sculptures. He got a scholarship at the Royal Academy of Arts. He's probably too modest to have told you."

"You're right."

So that was what he was studying in London! When he had mentioned studying in London, she had assumed that he meant learning English. Now everything made sense. He had left the job in the hotel because it required breakfast and lunch shifts, which clashed with his lessons. The restaurant where he worked now was only open in the evenings.

Why hadn't he told her? Perhaps because she had never asked.

"So he has an artist's hut?"

Now that Alice had exposed herself, she might as well fish for as much information as she could.

"Yes. I understand it's one of those shacks where shepherds find shelter in bad weather. He's fixed it up and filled it with art supplies. When he goes there, you never know when he'll come back or in what state of mind. He forgets everything, even to eat, sleep and drink. When he returns, he's either feverish with excitement or depressed. Either way, the aura is so strong that you can tell even before he comes into the house. When he's low, even his Vespa sounds depressed, I kid you not!"

Alice had not yet seen this side of Paolo and it intrigued her.

Paolo the sculptor. Did he sculpt with life models who posed naked for him up in his hut?

She chased this thought away as well as the unjustified jealousy that had come with it.

Now that she knew about his art, she could agree that there was a certain artistic vibe to the man.

Vittoria was right about the "aura".

Alice was still awake when, just after midnight, she heard the low rumble of Paolo's Vespa. It sounded like a dejected moan, just as Vittoria had said.

What had gone wrong? Had inspiration eluded him or the material not obeyed to his chisel?

She wanted to ask him and offer him her shoulder to cry on but she couldn't: she wasn't his real girlfriend.

Only when she heard Paolo click off the light switch in his room did she finally fall asleep.

CHAPTER 17

The butcher's shop opened at eight in the morning and Paolo and Alice were parked in front of the shop at 7.59. Despite the late night the day before, Paolo had woken up at dawn.

He had made no progress in his work. Gus's sculpture was still tightly wrapped inside its block of stone and would not emerge any time soon.

He didn't even know which block of stone that would be. Until inspiration struck, he couldn't do anything.

The bags under Alice's eyes told him that she hadn't slept much more either. She must be tense about today's meetings.

He couldn't imagine how it might feel to discover that he had been adopted and to have to look for his birth parents.

They watched the butcher's electric roller shutters rise with a lot of clanging and whirring noises.

"What if we walk into the shop and Simona is there?" Alice fretted.

"We don't have to go in. We can turn around and go home. Nobody will know. You can call this trip a holiday and spend the rest of your time in Calabria at the beach." He wouldn't mind spending time at the beach with her.

"I can't. I've got to find my birth mother, both for myself and for her," she replied, her jaw set.

"Have you considered that she might have changed her mind and not want to see you anymore?"

"Then she can send me away. I

won't rest if I haven't given us both a chance."

"As you wish."

As soon as the butcher's glass door was unlocked, Paolo and Alice walked into the shop.

Two men were carrying trays of meat out of the fridges and laying them on the display cabinets.

"How can I help?" the older of the two asked them.

"Hello, we're looking for Filomena Caracciolo," Paolo said.

"That's my daughter. Why are you looking for her?"

"We're seeking information on someone who lived in her old home."

"Are you *carabinieri*?" the butcher asked suspiciously.

"Not at all. We are searching for long-lost family who used to live at your daughter's old address."

The man nodded. Family was important in cities as in villages. "She's at the New Condera," he said gravely.

"Where is that?" Paolo asked but, just then, a customer had walked into the shop and the butcher greeted them.

Paolo and Alice would have to find it on their phone maps.

"Thank you for all you're doing to help me," Alice said to Paolo once they were out of the shop and he had relayed to her the butcher's information. "I don't know what I'd do without you. I hope you don't mind taking me to this other place."

He was tempted to say that he did mind, that this search wasn't a good idea. Her birth mother might not appreciate being found. In addition, she might be a very different woman from the one Alice expected her to be.

Alice might not like what she discovered about her origins and he didn't want her to get hurt.

But she looked at him with such

gratitude that he didn't have the heart to refuse. He inserted the address into his phone's satnav and they set off again.

CHAPTER 18

The road was lined with flower-sellers. People were going in and out of a large gate with bunches of flowers. "What sort of place is this?"

"I'm afraid it looks like a cemetery."

"Was the butcher trying to tell us that his daughter has passed away?" Alice remembered that he had looked a little sombre.

"I'll find out."

Paolo disappeared into the guardhouse and Alice stayed by the entrance, admiring some funeral monuments in the shape of small chapels.

He reappeared shaking his head. "Her grave is over there."

It made sense. The house had been sold to the woman with the dogs because the previous owner had died.

"Poor man. We should have never asked him about his daughter. She couldn't have been very old when she died. How sad!"

It was so disappointing. How were they to find out more about Simona? The butcher might know something but it felt indelicate to go back and quiz him. "What are we going to do now?"

Paolo scratched his chin. "While we think about it, let's go and say a prayer on her grave."

They followed the directions of the cemetery's guard to a beautiful, white marble tombstone with carved angels spreading their wings towards the sky.

Alice hadn't prayed for a long time and wasn't sure how to do it. She closed her eyes.

"Dear God…"

Paolo nudged her. "Look at the dates."

She opened her eyes to find the Filomena Caracciolo buried there had been more than ninety years old. "She can't be the butcher's daughter!"

"May I help you?" a woman asked them. She was holding a bunch of flowers and looking at them suspiciously.

Paolo talked to her and they chuckled. What were they saying? Alice wished she could understand more Italian.

"Alice, this is Filomena Caracciolo, daughter of the butcher. She is here to put flowers on her grandmother's grave. Filomena was named after her grandmother."

What a relief! After paying their respects to Filomena senior, they explained to Filomena junior the reason for their visit.

She told them there hadn't been anyone called Simona while she lived there but she had only bought the property ten years prior. There might have been a Simona living there before her time. She gave them the previous owner's contact details.

"We were lucky that she still kept those details in her phone," Alice commented once they were back in the car.

"I think she still has dealings with him. I understand that he's a local businessman."

They parked in front of a dingy-looking café. The buildings around it bore graffiti and weeds grew in the cracks of the walls. As soon as they got out of the car, Alice felt the eyes of the people in the café, all men, pinned on them. It didn't feel a welcoming place.

She reached for Paolo's hand. "I don't like the vibes of this place."

"Let me do the talking," he said.

Of course her poor Italian meant that there was no other way.

The café only displayed a couple of stale-looking pizzas with hardened cheese on top and a fly flitting between them. There was no aroma of coffee, no hissing and gurgling of coffee machines.

"It doesn't look like they do much trade here," she whispered.

"They probably trade in other things."

Alice shuddered.

A group of men were playing cards around a plastic table. All had stopped and were scanning them in an unwelcoming way.

One, wearing an apron, addressed Paolo.

Paolo looked relaxed and confident as he spoke but Alice felt the tension in his hand and felt guilty. She had put him in this difficult situation.

At a point in the conversation, one of the men stood up and banged a fist on the table, sending the playing cards flying. He growled at Paolo. Alice picked up only some of the words. *Polizia. Giornalisti.* Was the man accusing Paolo of being police or an investigative journalist?

"Wait," she said in Italian, taking a step forward.

From their frowns she realised that these men weren't used to a woman speaking without an invitation.

"We are not police or investigators. I'm just looking for my mother," she said in her shaky Italian.

The cat was out of the bag now and there was no way to put it back. She had offered the men all she had—the truth.

The man who had growled at Paolo now fixed her intently as if trying to decide whether she was telling the truth. He beckoned them both with a finger.

Alice and Paolo exchanged a glance and followed him to the back of the café.

The room at the back of the café didn't look like a food preparation area nor anything else that ought to belong to a café. Filing cabinets lined the walls all the way to the ceiling. How much paperwork were Italian small businesses required to keep, she wondered.

They sat down at a small table, facing the man who started speaking.

"He's saying that—" Paolo began but the man made a sharp gesture with his hand to instruct him to stop translating.

Alice had to resign herself just to studying the men's facial expressions and listening to sentences that didn't mean anything to her. All the while, curiosity tortured her.

Eventually, Paolo scribbled a name

and an address on the back of his hand.

The man got up which was a clear sign that their time was over.

"*Grazie*," Alice said, smiling.

He didn't smile back. He gave the impression of being someone who had forgotten how to smile.

CHAPTER 19

As they walked out of the café the card players were all silent. Again Alice felt their eyes boring into her and Paolo. "Tell me everything," she begged as soon as they had got into the car.

"Not here."

He turned on the engine and pulled out.

"Why?"

"I'm not sure you'll keep a poker face when I tell you what he said and those guys are still watching us."

They drove until they got to the seafront, where he pulled over. "I think this is safe enough."

"What's all this about?"

"You might have understood that the guy is quite shady," Paolo began.

"I suspected that."

"He buys and lets properties, possibly as a way to launder dirty money."

"Please, tell me I'm not related to him!"

"I don't think you are."

She breathed out with relief.

"He confirmed what Filomena told us—that he owned the property and let it before he sold it to her. I asked him if he remembered the tenants he had twenty-seven years ago. He didn't even have to look into his rental logbooks to tell me that it was a family with two daughters. That's why he believed you when you told him that you were looking for your mother: one of those girls was pregnant."

A girl. A teenage mother. That was why she had given her away! Until now she had imagined Simona as a woman, young perhaps but never a girl.

A pang of sympathy and compassion squeezed her heart.

"Did he tell you how old she was?"

"No. He might not even have met her."

"How does he know she was pregnant?"

"Now comes the bit that will make you angry. The girls' parents begged him to release them from their rental contract before its expiry. They wanted to move so that their daughter could have the baby somewhere people didn't know them. He refused."

"What a rat! What happened to the family? To me?"

"The parents stayed in the house and sent the girl off to give birth somewhere else."

"Poor Simona! Where was she sent?"

"He didn't know but he searched his books and has given me the family's surname, Latta, and the forwarding address they gave him when they moved out. It was about twenty-five years ago so prepare yourself for the possibility that it might come to nothing."

"Can we go now? How far is it?"

He pointed to the mountains. "It's a village in the middle of the Aspromonte mountains. I'm sorry but it's not a trip for tonight."

"That's okay," she said, trying to hide her disappointment. "We can go tomorrow or another day."

Rationally she knew that finding her birth mother would take time. But they were so close now!

She couldn't expect Paolo to put as much time into the search for Simona as her. He had his work to do and a family to be with. He had been missed last night at supper. She should not be so selfish.

He cleared his throat. "This address

is in a village in the mountains. In such places everyone knows everyone else's business."

"Isn't that a good thing? Anyone will be able to tell us where to find Simona," she said, confused by his sombre expression.

"Yes, but if we go there and start stirring up secrets from the past, someone is going to get hurt. I don't think we should do it."

"I've got to find Simona! I wouldn't live with myself if I didn't try every possible route. I'll be discreet. In fact, you don't need to worry because you'll be the one doing all the talking."

"Like just now at the café? That was very brave but you could have said the wrong thing."

She hadn't. Her Italian was improving.

"I won't say a word, I promise." She kissed her forefinger and middle finger back and front as she had seen

Paolo's younger cousins do when they were playing a game and were asked to swear compliance to the rules.

He ran a hand over his face.

Alice hated to see him so tortured. "Don't worry, I'll go on my own. You have work to do and family to be with."

"We'll go tomorrow morning as soon as we get up," he responded.

"No, Paolo. You don't want to do it and you have commitments. Stay and work."

"I can't work!" he roared, then took a deep steadying breath. "I'm sorry."

"No need."

She wanted to ask him about his work, perhaps help him offload some frustration, but he turned on the car's engine.

"Let's go home and plan tomorrow's trip," he suggested.

CHAPTER 20

Lia had insisted on making packed lunches for them. The focaccias filled with Parma ham and rocket leaves looked and smelled delicious.

It was going to be a long trip up on the mountains, deep inside the Aspromonte National Park. It was a good idea to take food along in case there wasn't anywhere to buy some.

Alice had looked at the map. They were going to travel through long stretches of mountain roads without towns or villages.

She felt bad at taking Paolo away from his family and work for what might be yet another full day.

She also felt bad at forcing him to drive the car yet again. The man loved his Vespa and she'd noticed he used it any time he wasn't with her.

If she could allow him to ditch the car today and ride the mountain roads on his Vespa, the trip might be less taxing to him.

While he was engaged in a heated debate with his mother over whether they should have provola cheese in the focaccias or not, Alice went out the front door and studied the Vespa.

She stroked the weathered leather seat. This bike was so different from the one her parents used to ride. Could she ride pillion without thinking about them?

She hopped on to the seat and imagined herself as Audrey Hepburn in "Roman Holiday". She didn't look anything like the famous actress but Paolo didn't resemble Gregory Peck, either, bar the cheeky smile.

Paolo appeared. "There you are! Changed your mind about my riding?"

"I think I'll give you a chance."

"You won't regret it."

They secured their lunches on to the Vespa's rack—Lia had won and the focaccias had provola, too—and Paolo straddled the bike and started the engine.

The sound made Alice's fear mount. No, she couldn't do this!

He must have read it on her face because immediately he killed the engine. "We can go by car if you're not sure."

She shook her head. She wanted to be able to do this.

"How about I take you to the end of the road and back so you see how it feels?" he suggested.

"Okay."

As soon as she sat behind him, her thighs pressed against his and her hands on his taut waist, she knew how it felt: too nice to be good for her!

They were spooned into each other, virtually hugging, and she forgot that they were on a motorbike with no protection from the gritty tarmac other than their clothes.

Paolo rode so slowly that it was a wonder he could keep balance. When he turned around at the end of the road she felt almost bereft.

"How was that?" he asked when they came to a stop.

"Let's ride up the mountains," she replied enthusiastically.

A smile crinkled his eyes.

It didn't take them long to leave Altavicia and start ascending the mountains. They passed fields of wheat, olive groves and vineyards, then the nature reserve began. Stretches of diss grass, broom and agave turned into forests of holm oak and strawberry tree. As they continued the climb, the air became cooler and beech and durmast formed patches of forest along the course of streams. Paolo rode steadily, filling Alice with enough confidence to take her eyes off the road and enjoy the breath-taking views of the sea and the island of Sicily beyond.

Eventually, the hairpins grew tighter and the sea was out of sight. Villages were nestled between dark green forests and weathered spurs of rock.

They stopped to drink at a spring that spurted out of the side of the road. The water came from a pipe and collected in a pretty fountain hewn in the rock.

"This water tastes so good!" she said, collecting the water in her cupped hands.

"Mountain water." He caught it in his mouth.

She enjoyed the journey so much

that, when they finally reached the village, she had forgotten they weren't mere tourists.

As they rode past the first houses, anxiety roiled in the pit of her stomach. Today she might finally meet Simona. She might be disappointed by her, rejected or denied.

Whatever happened, she knew she had to go through this or she would always wonder.

"Are you scared?" he asked her through their helmets as they climbed the steep, narrow streets.

"How can you tell?"

"You're holding on a lot tighter."

She let go of him and held on to the Vespa's seat instead, but he placed her arms back around his waist.

"I didn't say I didn't like it."

CHAPTER 21

Having Alice ride pillion behind him was more distracting than Paolo would have imagined: the feel of her arms around his waist and her chest pressing against his back when he used the brakes.

He couldn't afford distractions. She was giving him a chance to prove to her that riding with him wasn't a gamble with death, and he wanted to pass the test.

Their destination was a two-storey house at the end of a road.

"This is the place. Still happy for me to handle the conversation?"

"Yes, please, as we agreed. Besides, I'm too tense now that we're getting so close."

"Maybe not so close," he replied, noticing that the label on the doorbell read a different surname from "Latta".

He rang the bell anyway.

"Hello?" a woman called from the balcony above.

"Hello. We're looking for the Latta family. Do they live here?"

He hoped that the woman would come down so they wouldn't have to shout the rest of their conversation, but she didn't.

"No," the woman cried, shaking her head.

"Do you know anyone in the village called Latta?" he persisted.

From inside the house came the sound of a child whining. The woman clicked her tongue and threw her head back to indicate "No".

"What about the people who owned

the house before you? Were they called Latta?"

The child's whining had turned into full crying.

"I don't know, ask my neighbour. He knows everything!" the woman said scornfully then retreated into the house and closed the French doors.

"What did she say?" Alice asked.

Just as Paolo was relaying the disappointing conversation with the woman, the top half of the French shutters of the house next door opened and an old man peered out.

"Don't ask that one anything: she only moved here ten years ago. Who are you looking for?" he asked them in a thick local accent.

"The Latta family. We were told they used to live here many years ago."

"Why are you looking for them?"

The man was making clear that this conversation was going to be an exchange of information, not a donation.

"We think we might be long-lost family," Paolo said, keeping it as vague as he could.

"Ah!" The man raised his forefinger in the air and wagged it. "Listen to me. You don't want any more family than you're already cursed with. Family is trouble and strife. Better alone than in bad company, so goes the proverb."

Paolo smiled respectfully.

"Do you remember anyone called Latta living here?"

The man closed his eyes and thought. "Yes, I remember them."

Alice must have understood because she clasped her hands to her chest and smiled.

"They came from Reggio. Father, mother and one daughter."

"Was the daughter called Simona?"

"No. Cetta. I remember because all day long the mother shouted, 'Cetta do this'; 'Cetta do that.' The girl was bone lazy."

The landlord had told Paolo that the Lattas had two daughters. This could be Simona's family. Perhaps she never returned to the family after her "exile".

"Do you have any idea where they might be now?"

"No, they kept to themselves. They didn't go to church or to the market, they never went for a stroll in the square and didn't talk to anyone. If I don't know much about them, you can bet no one else in the village does."

Paolo didn't doubt this.

"Did they leave a forwarding address?"

"Not that I know of. They might have given it to the people who bought the house from them, the Mannoias."

"Do you know where we can find them?"

"The Mannoias? Of course."

"Where are they?"

"Everywhere." The man opened his arms as if to encompass the world.

"What's he saying?" Alice asked.

Her understanding of Italian was growing at impressive speed but the man's last answer didn't make sense to Paolo either. "I'm not sure." He looked up at the man. "Can you explain?"

"The Mannoias own half this village! But the branch of the family you're looking for owns the tobacconist's in the main square. The family bought the Lattas' house for their son who was getting married, but then he and his wife left for the city." The man shook his head.

They thanked him and said goodbye, then Paolo relayed to Alice the bits of the conversation she hadn't caught.

CHAPTER 22

"Please, don't tell me that today is the day when tobacconist shops are closed!" Alice called as they rode off.

"There could never be such a thing. Some people need tobacco more than they need food," he replied with a chuckle.

The tobacconist's was one of only three shops in the square. Paolo and Alice hadn't even taken off their helmets and the men sitting outside the café were already staring.

Theirs weren't hostile stares as in the last café, merely curious ones.

Inside the shop, a portly lady sat

behind the lottery machines.

"Hello. We're looking for the Mannoias," Paolo began.

"Why?"

"We need information about a family they bought a house from. The Lattas."

The woman's features hardened. "Are you police?"

"Nothing like that. We're long-lost family." Paolo raised his arms in innocence.

The woman's features relaxed. "We bought the house from the Lattas many years ago. It was for our son but then..."

Such a mournful expression crossed the woman's face that, if Paolo hadn't already heard the story, he would have guessed her son had died prematurely.

"He moved away," she finished.

"I'm sorry," Paolo said.

The woman nodded. "Yes, so it was us who bought the house from the

Lattas."

"Do you know where they moved next? Did they leave you a forwarding address?"

Even without looking at Alice he could sense her anticipation and hope.

"They did but I haven't got it anymore." The woman shrugged.

"Do you remember whereabout? The village or town?"

"It was in Reggio, that's all I remember."

That was a blow. Finding the Lattas in another village might have been possible without an address, but in Reggio there was no chance. This was the end of the line for their search.

Paolo thanked her and turned to Alice, dreading the task of translating the bad news, but she must have understood enough because she looked dejected.

"She doesn't know where they are, does she?"

Paolo shook his head. He wanted to comfort her with a hug but wasn't sure that she would appreciate it.

"What can we do now?"

"Best that we go home and think about it."

The truth was that he had already thought about it and had come to the conclusion that nothing could be done.

He wasn't going to say that to Alice. He had a feeling that, unless she came to that conclusion on her own, she would resist.

"Would you like me to take you home a different way? Show you some sights of Calabria?" he asked.

"I can't imagine better sights than the ones we've seen on the way up here," she replied.

He searched for words of comfort. "I'm sorry this hasn't worked out. Sometimes things don't go the way you hope for a reason. I know you wanted to find your birth mother but some people might be happier this way."

"Simona did want to know me. She wrote those letters," she said, her voice breaking.

"I was thinking of your parents. Have you thought that they might be a little jealous?"

Sadness clouded her face. "They are dead, Paolo."

He gasped. "Oh, I'm so sorry! How could I not have known that?"

"You couldn't. My parents died after you left the hotel. We know so little about each other."

He wrapped her hands in his. "Both of them?"

"It was a motorbike accident." She avoided his gaze.

"Oh, Alice!" He pulled her into his arms and she melted into him. Silent tears went through his T-shirt and touched his chest.

He wanted to turn into a shell

around her to protect her from pain and hurt. Now it made sense. "I should never have asked you to ride the Vespa with me."

"Not true. You have cured me. I enjoyed it," she said quietly, then pulled away a little. "Don't think I'm looking for my birth mother to replace my parents. They could never be replaced, even if I'm mad at them for keeping this secret from me. I just want to find more about my origins and the woman who gave birth to me."

"I understand." He tightened the hug and kissed the top of her head.

CHAPTER 23

They descended the mountains and headed back to Altavicia. The trees in the valleys, the rocks at the tops and even the birds in the sky looked a little less happy than on the way up, Alice decided.

She sighed inside her helmet. Was it true that they had run out of chances to find Simona?

Eventually, the road joined the coastline and ran along it. The Vespa slowed down and Paolo pulled over on the side of the road.

"Are we out of fuel?" she asked, worried about their lonely location.

"I'll have you know that I do not ever run out of fuel. No, I've stopped because we deserve a swim."

He was trying to cheer her up, she knew, which was very sweet, but she wasn't in the mood. "We have no swimsuits or towels with us."

"This isn't England. We don't need towels when it's warm enough to dry off in the wind. As for swimsuits, we can go in with our clothes on. Or, if you prefer, in the nude," he added with a look of mischief.

"No way! No skinny dipping, thank you very much!" she said, smiling.

But the thought was more exciting than she was willing to admit.

Paolo stepped off the Vespa and rocked it onto its stand despite the fact that Alice was still sitting on it.

He took off his helmet. "I'm going to have a swim. You can stay here and watch me or you can have fun, too."

The sea before them was turquoise

and lapis lazuli speckled with gold. Alice knew she couldn't go back to England having missed out on such an opportunity. "Fine, I'll come."

They locked their helmets securely on to the Vespa and scrambled down the rocky shore.

"The last one in the water is a loser!" Paolo shouted as soon as he was ahead of her.

"That's not fair, you've started before me!" she protested.

He laughed and leaped over the rocks with the agility of a mountain goat.

When he got to the waterline, Paolo pulled his T-shirt off his back and dropped it on the rocks. Alice tried not to be distracted by the sight of his bare torso.

"Wait, the tide will take away your T-shirt!" she warned, still trying to catch up with him.

He kicked off his shoes and

chuckled. "The tide is tiny here, not like in England. Come on!" He ran to the water's edge and dived straight in.

She took off her shoes but kept everything else on and jumped into the water after him. The water was only slightly cold, certainly not enough to take her breath away.

Something else did, though.

As Paolo resurfaced, shaking the water off his hair in a spray of sparkling droplets, his eyelashes looked even longer, his irises more golden, and his lips redder as they glittered with pearls of water. She had to dive underwater to stop herself staring.

There must have been a thermal vent because she found herself in a warmer layer of water which enveloped her like in an embrace. She turned around so that she was belly up and could look at the quivering surface from underneath.

The sun's rays pierced through the water's surface, shimmering and pulsating. The muffled sound of the water left her imagining that this must be what it was like to be in the womb.

Whose womb had protected her and nurtured her to life?

She chased the question away. She couldn't think about it now.

From the corner of her eye she saw Paolo swim underwater towards her. His hair was like a halo around him and bubbles came out of his grinning mouth. What was he going to do? Pull her feet? Tickle her? Kiss her?

No. The one time they had kissed it had been to show his family that they were together. What they were doing now, frolicking in the water like children, was real.

She didn't find out what he was about to do because she couldn't hold her breath any longer and had to resurface, spluttering and gasping.

A moment later, he resurfaced too.

"Race you to the buoy!" she said and set off quickly splashing as much as she could with her legs to hinder his progress.

Paolo must have hung back because she got to the fisherman's buoy first.

"I'm the king of the castle and you're the dirty rascal!" she chanted.

"How can I be dirty if I'm soaking in clean water?"

"After soaking, rinsing is needed," she said mischievously.

She started splashing him, to which he retaliated in kind. Alice hadn't had this much fun since her childhood.

When they eventually returned to the shore, driven by hunger, they stretched themselves onto the rocks to dry off, panting.

The sun tickled Alice's skin as it dried the water, leaving the salt. This felt like a holiday!

"It was a good idea to stop for a

swim," she admitted.

"But it's made me hungry," he replied. "Do we have any food left? No? Let's go home, then." He stood up and put on his T-shirt.

"Our shorts are still wet, though," Alice objected.

"Never mind. It's never damaged the Vespa's seat."

So this wasn't the first time Paolo had ridden his Vespa in wet clothes.

Whom had he taken on impromptu swims before? Rosaria? Other girls? The thought gave her a prick of jealousy but she chased it away. She had no claims over him, after all, and certainly no right to be jealous.

Their relationship was only a pretence. Paolo was being very kind to her, helping her in her search for Simona, but it was only because they had made a deal.

He was doing more than his fair share of the deal in the way he looked after her and cared about her feelings, an inner voice suggested.

She squashed the voice. Paolo was being a good friend, that was all.

A romantic relationship would never work out between them. He was a spur-of-the-moment man. Someone who hadn't thought twice about lying to his mother. He could not be trusted.

Alice had already been burned by people who had seemed trustworthy but had deceived her all the same. Her own parents.

***

On the return journey she made sure to sit as far back on the seat of the Vespa as safety allowed.

As Paolo had predicted, by the time they got home the wind had dried out their clothes.

At the gate, there was mail in the letterbox and Paolo pulled it out.

"A bill for Papà and a letter for Mamma," he said, flicking through them.

Alice peered over his shoulders. "Your mum hasn't taken the family surname. Sorry, I'm being nosy."

"No, women in Italy don't change their surnames when they marry. In fact, nobody can change their surname unless they have serious reasons to do so. The procedure isn't a simple one."

An idea flickered in Alice's mind. "Are you saying that, if Simona was born Latta, she would still be called that even if she had got married?"

"Absolutely."

Hope burst inside Alice like fireworks. "Then we can search her online, can't we?"

"There must be hundreds of Simona Lattas," Paolo warned.

"Let's try anyway."

She ran to her room, opened her laptop and typed frantically.

There were not hundreds of Simona Lattas. Alice found only a handful, and

one of them owned a confectionery workshop in Reggio Calabria.

CHAPTER 24

The shop's window was blocked with cardboard, a grubby fly curtain hung over the main door and the walls around it were graffitied with swear words. This was a far cry from the bright and shiny shop on a bustling street that Alice had imagined. An unpleasant frisson ran down her back.

What if Simona, too, wasn't as Alice had pictured her?

She had imagined her birth mother as an older version of herself physically. In every other way, she had seen her like Paolo's mother—exuberant, warm and welcoming.

There had been nothing warm and cosy about the woman with the barking dog, the unsavoury landlord and the distrustful villagers she had met in her search for Simona. Was her birth mother going to disappoint her as well?

Now that the answers to all her questions about Simona were within reach, Alice wasn't sure she wanted to know them anymore.

"Are you okay?" Paolo asked, taking her hand. His was warm and comforting and it infused her with courage.

She nodded.

They walked up to the door. From inside came the whirring of a machine, perhaps a dough mixer, and the faint smell of warm sugar. Was it a good omen or would this turn out to be the witch's gingerbread house from the fairy tale?

A phone rang inside the shop and

Alice jumped. It felt like an alarm warning her to keep away.

"I can't do this. Let's go home," she said, recoiling.

"Are you sure?"

The phone kept on ringing, sending more adrenaline coursing through her body.

"Yes. I'm so sorry."

"Don't be."

"I've wasted your time."

"I've enjoyed spending it with you."

She smiled wanly. They jumped back on the Vespa and rode home.

Paolo was being very nice about it but, all through the journey, Alice thought about her failure. He had been right when he told her that looking for her birth mother was a bad idea and it would hurt people, including herself.

That evening, Paolo's mother cooked another feast. When Alice happily accepted seconds of the spaghetti with anchovies and breadcrumbs, Lia told her, in Italian as usual, that she would teach her the recipe. It was very simple.

Since Alice's arrival, Lia had been speaking to her in Italian as if there were no language difference between them.

At first Alice had taken it as a reproach for allegedly dating Paolo without bothering to learn the language. Later she had taken it as Lia trying to teach her the language. Now she realised that it was neither of those things. Lia had talked to her in Italian because she wanted desperately to communicate with her. Italian was the only way to do this and Lia wouldn't let obstacles hold her back.

Her doggedness had given Alice so much practice that her wish was coming true: Alice could understand simple Italian.

"*Grazie,*" Alice replied, gratefully.

She didn't mean just for the offer to teach her the recipe.

After dinner, it was Alice and Paolo's turn to wash up. While they were alone at the sinks, he whispered into her ear.

"I think it would be easier for you and Simona if you made your first contact by email or phone. Turning up at her shop out of the blue might be too much for both of you."

He hadn't given up on her, then.

"I'm sorry, I should have gone into the shop while we were there. It was cowardly of me to chicken out like that."

"It wasn't cowardly. It was human."

"Paolo, if I had been brave enough to walk into that shop, the whole business would have been done and dusted by now. You would be working on your sculpture instead of thinking of ways to help me. I'm taking up so much of your time that I'm ashamed." She rubbed the plate she held so vigorously with the soapy sponge that some bubbles landed on her cheek.

He wiped them off but, instead of removing his finger when he was done, he let it linger on her cheek. What had started as a bubble-wiping gesture was turning into a caress.

His gaze roved from her cheek to her lips and stayed there.

If Paolo was faking the notion that he wanted to kiss her, he was doing it well. But what was the point of it if nobody was watching?

Alice realised this wasn't part of their fake relationship. It was authentic.

Her skin tingled. The most startling thing was that she wanted to kiss him, too.

"More plates coming through," Vittoria said, bursting into the kitchen with a pile of dirty dishes. "Oh, sorry!"

She deposited them quickly on the table and all but ran out again, like someone who has interrupted an intimate moment.

So, Alice hadn't dreamt it: other people could see it, too.

Paolo stepped back. Confusion and worry marbled his face. Clearly, he hadn't meant for this moment to happen.

The thought saddened her.

That evening, Alice didn't join the family watching a movie in the sitting room, even if it would have been good for her language studies. She and Paolo would have been expected to sit together on the sofa and such a level of proximity was more than she could bear after what had happened earlier.

There could be nothing more than friendship between them. If Paolo was falling in love with her, she could not rely on him to take action to stop them getting too close with each other. And that was something which must be avoided.

CHAPTER 25

Another email from Gus asking for progress. How long would Paolo be able to fend him off? Paolo should be holing up in his hut and working on the commission at this moment. Instead, he was sitting on Alice's bed ready to help her with her all-important phone call. And he didn't regret it for a second.

He loved spending time with her. There wasn't a moment in the day when he didn't think of her. The only regret he had right now was about not pulling her onto his lap and kissing her.

What was happening to him? He felt like he was falling in love but that just couldn't be. After all, he didn't believe in love anymore.

Last night, wiping the bubbles off her cheek at the sinks while they washed up, he had almost lost control of himself and kissed her. He must not let their fake relationship become a real one. He had nothing to offer a woman.

"I'm ready," Alice told him, breaking into his thoughts.

For a moment, he forgot about the phone call and imagined she meant she was ready for a kiss.

"Me too." Then he realised.

The mobile phone was set to *speaker*. It took only a couple of rings before a woman's voice answered.

"Hello?"

Paolo couldn't imagine the emotions going through Alice at hearing for the first time the voice of the woman who could be her birth mother.

"Hello?" the woman asked again.

"Are you okay?" he mouthed.

Alice shook her head. She wanted to do this herself—he mustn't try to help her against her will.

"I'm tired of your games," the woman at the other end of the phone said. "I'm not going to be intimidated and I've already reported you to the police!"

Someone must have been pestering her with nuisance calls, then. Or intimidating ones.

What kind of life did this woman have? With what sort of people did she mix?

Paolo wanted to end the phone call and take Alice away from this woman, protect her from harm. But he had no right to do that.

All he could do was hope that this wasn't her birth mother after all.

THE ITALIAN FAKE DATE

Alice recovered herself. "Hello. I'm looking for Simona," she responded in shaky Italian and an even shakier voice.

"Speaking," the woman replied cautiously.

"Can you speak English?"

"A little bit. Who are you?" Simona asked in English.

"I'm Alice Baker."

There was silence at the other end, then she spoke.

"Are you...?" Simona's voice was breaking a little.

"You probably know me better as Francesca."

"*Santo Cielo*, good heavens!" she said breathlessly. "*La mia bambina*, my baby!" She burst into sobs.

Alice began crying, too. Paolo put his arm around her shoulders and wiped her tears with a tissue.

"Can I meet you, please?" Simona pleaded in English.

The only thing emerging from Alice's throat were loud sobs so Paolo answered for her. "We'll come to your shop. Give us a couple of hours."

"Who are you?" Simona asked, sounding tense.

"I'm her boyfriend."

Why had he said that? There were no chances of Simona ever meeting his own family. He could have told her the truth—that he and Alice were just friends—but he hadn't. Even more surprising was how what he told her didn't feel like a lie.

"Please, bring her safely to me. Don't have an accident," Simona begged.

"We won't."

He ended the call then pulled a sobbing Alice onto his lap and held her until she had calmed down. Why did holding her in his arms feel so right?

Eventually, she calmed and looked up at him with a watery smile.

"When I asked for translation help, I wasn't expecting the full service. Thank you," she managed.

"I'm only doing what a good boyfriend would do," he wanted to say but didn't. It couldn't be right that their fictional relationship was bleeding into real life.

CHAPTER 26

There was new graffiti on the wall of the shop. It was a swear word that could only apply to a woman so it must have been intended for Simona. Paolo hoped Alice's Italian was too shaky to translate.

Clearly, Simona had upset someone, and that someone was troubling her with nuisance calls and graffiti. What if Simona brought problems into Alice's life?

Should he have sabotaged her quest for her birth mother as he had originally intended? No. Alice would have never given up; it would have just taken her longer.

Maybe Alice needed Simona. Certainly, he was sure Simona had everything to gain from having Alice in her life.

He chained the Vespa to a lamppost. In this part of town you wouldn't leave your possessions unattended and unsecured.

Unlike the surroundings, the smell coming from the shop was heavenly.

Paolo took Alice's helmet from her and threaded it through his arm with his own. She walked forward shakily and stopped in front of the shop.

"You're coming in, aren't you?"

"Of course. But you'll be fine."

"Promise that, if she speaks in Italian, you'll translate everything she says. Even if it something that could hurt me."

"I promise."

He parted the fly curtain. A delicious smell of baking wafted straight into his nostrils.

The shop was bare: there were only a couple of plastic chairs lined against the wall and a counter with notebook and a pen.

Paolo glanced at the open pages. It looked like an order book but most of the orders were crossed out. That didn't bode well.

At the back of the room were double doors which had been propped open. Paolo glimpsed steel tables and units. That must be the actual workshop.

"Hello?" Alice called.

A small dark woman shot out of the double doors. Her apron was askew, dark curls had escaped from her hairnet and her eyes and nose were red with recent tears.

She stopped and scanned Alice with her mouth slightly open and eyes wide. What was she thinking as she watched her grown-up child for the first time?

Did she see herself in Alice? What about the biological father?

Simona cupped her cheeks with her hands and murmured in Italian.

"My baby girl!"

She pulled Alice into a hug and they cried in each other's arms. When they emerged, Alice had a streak of powdered sugar on her cheek.

"I look like you!" Alice said, surprised.

"I'm sorry," Simona replied with a smile.

Paolo didn't think she had anything to be sorry about. To him Alice looked perfect.

"I had lost hope of ever seeing you again," Simona told her, tears bobbing up again. "I don't hold it against your mum. I might have done the same. Does she know that you've come here?"

Alice's eyes darkened. "She's dead. Both my parents are dead."

"Oh, I'm sorry! Is this why you've looked for me?"

"I didn't know I had been adopted until my parents died."

"They never told you." Simona nodded. "Have something to eat."

She led them into her workshop where she had laid out a selection of chocolate cakes, apricot squares, pistachio and ricotta parcels.

"There are more in the oven, which I made when you told me you were coming."

Just like Paolo's own mum. Feeding people must be her language of love. His last reserves against Simona crumbled away.

He and Alice sat on the stools Simona offered them and tucked into the sweet feast while Simona told them her story and Paolo translated for Alice.

She was sixteen when she got pregnant and her parents wanted her to terminate the pregnancy. Desperate to keep the baby, she asked a childless English couple holidaying next door to adopt her.

Simona had imagined they'd come back every summer with her baby and she could see her but, after the adoption, the couple didn't set foot in Reggio Calabria again. Hence the desperate letters Alice had found in their loft.

"I don't hold it against your parents. I wasn't respecting their privacy and their rights. I was very young and could only see my own needs. I'm thankful that they kept those letters. If they hadn't, you would have never reached me," she added.

"Ask her about my father, Paolo."

"I think it's too soon. Give her time to recover from the shock of meeting you," he replied but Simona must have understood.

"You can ask me but you won't

believe the answer."

CHAPTER 27

Alice watched a blob of tiramisu fall from Paolo's mouth into his plate. "I don't understand," she said.

"Your biological father is Luigi Felice," Simona repeated.

"How did you know him?" Paolo asked.

Thankfully, the conversation had switched to English so Alice could follow it. At least, the letter of it. The meaning was still a mystery. Who was this guy and why was his name vaguely familiar?

Simona sat on a stool, crossed her knees and threaded her fingers over them.

"We were classmates," she said, looking dreamily into the distance. "We were both sixteen and we fell hard for each other. We were young and naïve. We didn't know what we were doing until, one day, we discovered that I was pregnant. As soon as our parents found out what we'd done, they forbade us to see each other and sent Luigi away to Rome. I believe it was there he started studying music."

"Who is Luigi Felice?" Alice begged.

Simona and Paolo looked at her as if she had asked who the Pope was.

"He's the tenor who sang on your first night in Altavicia," Paolo explained.

Alice's own mouth gaped. She should have paid more attention to the concert instead of messing about with Paolo and bags of sweets. She didn't even remember what the man looked like but she remembered his voice. Oh, she could never forget those velvety notes that had moved her to the point of tears.

Was it talent and skill that had touched her heart or had there been a more subconscious connection, perhaps?

"Are you back in touch with each other?" Alice asked.

"No. There were no mobile phones back then and I had no idea where to find him. After he'd become famous I thought he wouldn't want to have anything to do with me. I didn't want him to think that I was an opportunist, after his fame and money. For me it's enough to know that things have turned out well for him. I could never have forgiven myself if I had ruined his life."

She must have really loved him, Alice decided. "What happened to you?"

"I was sent to my aunt's pasticceria

where I learnt to make confectionery. I haven't got a husband or a family of my own but I love my job, which is more than most people can say. Love it so much that I'm sticking with it through thick and thin!" She gestured vaguely in the direction of the shop's entrance.

"Is the shop doing well?" Alice asked tentatively.

She had no idea how it could stay afloat without a sign over the door and displays in the window, here on a street with minimal footfall.

"This isn't a shop, it's a workshop. I don't sell directly to the public but to shops, hotels and restaurants. I have fewer customers than a high street shop would but each one of them orders a lot and regularly. Or they used to. Enough about me. Tell me all about you."

Alice tried to condense twenty-seven years of her life into a few sentences but Simona was full of questions.

Some of her mannerism and gestures were uncannily familiar. The way she laughed, the way she narrowed her eyes when she didn't understand something, the way she bit her lip when she wasn't happy. Simona was a strange mixture of familiar and alien and Alice was spellbound.

Hours went by. When Simona's phone rang and she went next door to take the call, Alice remembered that Paolo had work to do and she had been taking up his time.

"We should go home now," she told him.

He put a finger to his lips to signal to her to be quiet. Was he eavesdropping into Simona's phone conversation?

When Simona returned, she looked a little drained. Alice knew it was time to leave and let Paolo and Simona get on with their work.

She gathered the empty plates. "We should go home now but I'd like us to meet again."

"I hope so." Simona's eyes grew shiny again. "Just one thing: you should try to meet your father. I think he would like to see you. He wanted me to keep you."

Alice felt a knot in her throat, thinking of the sixteen-year-old who wanted his baby.

"When he heard that my parents were pressing me for a termination, Luigi asked me to run away with him."

Alice sat down again to listen.

"We were going to elope. We had money for two train tickets to Catanzaro and two slices of pizza from the baker. The plan was that we'd get married and he would find work while I looked after the baby. We had no idea where we were going to live—most likely we'd end up sleeping on park benches and under bridges for a while—but we were determined to do this to save the baby. You. So, if you're thinking of making contact with him, I'd say do it!"

Tears pricked the back of Alice's eyes. "Won't he think that I'm after his money and fame?"

"If he hasn't changed too much from the boy I fell in love with, no. He'll be delighted to meet you."

"What happened to your plans to elope?"

"Our parents found out. I'm not sure what happened at Luigi's end but I got locked in my bedroom for a few days. When my parents finally let me out, Luigi's family had moved to Rome and had taken him with them." Her voice trembled.

Alice hugged her and they stayed together in a long embrace.

"Are you angry with me for giving you away?" Simona whispered.

"No. I'm thankful that you saved my

life."

Simona let out a breath that she might have been holding for twenty-seven years.

CHAPTER 28

It was a silent journey back to Altavicia. Alice's head swam with Simona's revelations. How could she be cross with Simona for giving her away when she had fought for Alice's life with courage and love?

She admired her father, too—a penniless teenage boy willing to take on responsibilities beyond his years to look after the family he had started.

She didn't resent her parents anymore. They could have destroyed Simona's letters but, instead, they had saved them in the heart-shaped box together with her baby things.

Had they intended to show them to her one day? Maybe they just hadn't had the heart to burn them. Alice would never know.

Yes, it had been wrong to keep her adoption a secret, but now that she knew how much Simona had loved her and wanted her she could understand why they might have felt threatened.

Simona and Luigi's story was tragic but her parents' was, too. They had been the pair who had stayed up at night when she was sick, who had taken her to violin lessons and dealt with her dramas with friendships.

They had been there for her every day and had brought her up with love.

As all resentments seeped out of her, Alice felt lighter.

***

Paolo manoeuvred the Vespa through the half-open gate and parked it in the shade of a pine tree. It must be just after midday so he still had time to go to his hut and work. Simona and Luigi's tragic love story had sparked a glimmer of inspiration inside him but first he must make sure Alice was okay.

Her hair was mussed by the helmet but her eyes were radiant with happiness. She looked so beautiful that it took all his willpower not to scoop her up and kiss her.

"If you want to meet... the man," he said, looking over his shoulders in case anyone was listening, "I'll help you."

"Thank you but you've already done more than your fair share of the deal."

The deal. These days, he often forgot about the deal. Helping Alice had become a natural thing to do and their fake relationship didn't feel fake anymore.

"I haven't. You're still pretending to be my girlfriend so I should still help you find your biological parents."

"I was right!" Vittoria popped up from behind the pittosporum hedge.

Paolo had forgotten that this was his sister's favourite sunbathing spot.

"I knew you weren't boyfriend and girlfriend for real!"

"Clever you. Now keep it to yourself."

She planted her fists on her hips and cocked her head. "Or? What will you do?"

"Please, Vittoria, don't give us grief."

"Why are you doing this? Is it a ruse to make Rosaria jealous so that she realises that she's still in love with you and ditches Marcello?"

"No! You're way off."

"Good, because I didn't think you were still in love with her. You can't be when you're obviously smitten with Alice."

Paolo would have brushed the comment off if it hadn't rung true. Yes, he was smitten with her.

He glanced at Alice in alarm. Had

she understood? She knew a lot more Italian now.

Thankfully, she looked confused. "What's going on?" she asked when she saw him looking at her.

"I'll tell you later."

"Will you?" Vittoria challenged him, wagging her finger. "I hope you are going to tell her everything because I don't know who you're trying to trick with your fake relationship. You're only deceiving yourselves."

"Don't say a word to Mamma, please."

"Ah, so you're doing this for her. You're making a big mistake," Vittoria said, shaking her head.

It irked him that she was speaking to him as if he was a naughty child when he was her older brother. "Then that would be my mistake, not yours."

She smiled impishly. It was a smile that didn't promise any compliance but, in fact, the opposite.

"What do you want in exchange for your silence?" he asked finally.

"I want you to tell Alice that you're in love with her." With that Vittoria turned around and lay back down on her sun lounger.

"What was that all about?" Alice asked when they were alone inside.

"She has heard us talk about the deal. She knows we're not actually boyfriend and girlfriend."

"Was that all? You seemed to talk for ages."

He hesitated. Vittoria's words were ringing in his ears. "Tell Alice that you're in love with her." No, he couldn't do it. This wasn't the place and time. He had just argued with his sister and he was in a stinking mood. Besides, he couldn't tell a woman his feelings for her just because his sister had strong-armed him into it. "She was just being annoying."

Alice seemed to be waiting for him

to give her more detail but he didn't and he was grateful that she didn't press him.

Instead, she smiled. "I guess that's a younger sibling's job, isn't it?"

"Quite. You're lucky to be an only child," he said.

"I would rather have the annoyance than the loneliness."

Her face clouded with sadness and he wished he hadn't made the remark.

In the end, Paolo decided that withholding information from Alice and arguing with Vittoria had banished his artistic inspiration and didn't go to the hut.

CHAPTER 29

That night, family suppertime was a little tense. To be more accurate, Paolo was tense. Everyone else was actually behaving normally except Vittoria, who kept darting glances at him and made him feel like there was an unexploded bomb in the centre of the table.

After supper, she walked into his room and sat in the chair next to his desk.

"It was fun to watch you sweat," she told him without malice.

"You are evil, little sister," he said flatly from the bed where he was lying with a book.

"I won't tell Mamma and Papà about you and Alice if you do it."

"I will. After Alice has gone home." He crossed his arms behind his head.

"She'll be sad."

Did she mean their mother or Alice? Surely the former.

"But I guess not half as sad as you will be when Alice leaves," she continued.

"Stop it, Vittoria."

"I'm guessing that you haven't shared your feelings with Alice yet. Why aren't you two together? Is it her? Has she got a boyfriend back in London, a real one?"

"No."

"Then it's you who's the problem. You should be kissing her for real, when no one is watching, not when a table full of people asks you!"

"It was you who shouted 'kiss' on her first day, wasn't it?" Paolo growled.

"Yes, it was. It would never have been a problem for you two if you were together for real. Instead, I saw the alarm on your face, Paolo. I knew immediately that she couldn't possibly be your real girlfriend or you would never have been embarrassed by a public kiss. I still can't work out why you're keeping up the pretence, though."

"To make Mamma happy."

Vittoria pushed down the head of the nodding dog on his desk. "And who makes you happy?"

"I don't..." He was about to say "deserve" but it sounded like self-pity. "I don't need happiness."

"Rubbish!" Vittoria jumped to her feet and started pacing the room. "I know what your problem is."

"I haven't got a problem."

She laughed wryly. "Oh, you do! You think that, because Rosaria left you for Marcello, you aren't good enough for anyone to have as a partner."

"Enough, Vittoria! I didn't ask for a psychoanalysis session." He got up from the bed and went to the door but Vittoria wasn't leaving.

"You're torturing yourself with this fake relationship, Paolo. What gave you this absurd idea of pretending you were together?" she persisted.

"It started with a misunderstanding with our mother."

"And you've carried it so far that now you look at Alice like a love-sick puppy but still won't make her your girlfriend for real? It's ridiculous."

Did he really look at Alice like a love-sick puppy? He must keep a better check on himself.

"We all want to see you happy, big brother, but for real." She play-punched his arm and walked out of his room.

CHAPTER 30

Alice was sitting with her laptop at the balcony of her room. The sun had just peeped over the tops of the mountains and already it felt warm.

Luigi Felice's website showed several photos of him. Alice studied them carefully. He looked younger than she had imagined but if he had been sixteen when she was born, he must be forty-three. Shockingly young to be her father.

He had her eyes and her nose, she decided.

There was a knock on her door.

"Come in."

Paolo opened the door and peeped in. She closed the laptop. "I was just looking at Luigi Felice's website. Unfortunately there are only the contact details of his agent. I don't know how I would explain to his agent why I need to get in touch with Luigi."

"No need. He lives just down the road."

"Are you serious?" She sat up.

"Absolutely. The reason he gave a free concert in Altavicia is that he considers himself an Altavician. When he was a child, he used to spend his holidays at his grandparents' here. He loves this village and he's bought a second home just outside the village. When he's not touring around the world he comes to stay. In fact, I think he's there right now."

"Do you know where it is?"

Paolo laughed. "Of course, everyone in Altavicia does. I'll take you."

"Just like that? We can't just turn

up."

"We can try. Are you ready?"

She was dressed simply in shorts and a T-shirt. She decided she wasn't going to dress up for Luigi Felice just because he was a famous person.

"I'm ready," she said, standing up.

"Shall we walk? It's not far."

"Sure."

They hadn't even left the village when Alice started feeling the heat. It was only mid-morning but the sun was already baking down on them, the tarmac and the oleander bushes that lined the sides of the road but were too small to provide shade.

Eventually, the pavement disappeared and there was only a dusty road flanked by the walls of small properties or the barbed wire fences of the fields.

In the distance was the sea. Alice would have given anything to dive in and cool down. Sweat dripped down her temples and the dust from the road stuck to it. Far from arriving at the tenor's house dressed in her best she would be caked in sweat and dust, too. Oh, well. This would be a good test of her biological father's acceptance of her.

Despite Simona's words, Alice wasn't sure Luigi Felice would be happy to see her. The starry-eyed teenager might well have been ready to sacrifice his future for his girlfriend and their baby but the adult man might feel differently now. Wealth, fame and success tended to change people and Luigi Felice had achieved all three.

After all, had he made any attempt to find out what had happened to Alice? Or Simona? It sounded like he hadn't been in touch with her since their traumatic separation.

"There it is," Paolo said, pointing to a large villa with elegant arches.

He frowned surveying the high, rough-textured walls, CCTV at every corner and the gate firmly shut. There were no gaps for curious eyes.

"The way people talk about him in the village I thought his place would be a little more welcoming," Paolo commented, checking out an intercom at the gate.

"I guess he has to avoid the paparazzi," Alice replied, feeling a little protective of her biological father.

"We can ring the intercom, anyway."

"What are we going to say?"

"That Simona Latta sent you."

"Can you handle this, please?" Alice begged.

"No problem."

He pressed the button and a woman answered in Italian. Alice understood that Paolo asked to speak to Luigi Felice, gave his name and mentioned Simona.

Clearly the woman had never heard about Simona, which wasn't surprising. She told him to ring or email Luigi first but she didn't supply his contact details.

Of course it was never going to be easy to get in touch with a music star.

"I hope we haven't made trouble for him by mentioning Simona," Alice fretted. "Do you think the woman who answered the intercom was his wife or partner?"

"He doesn't have one. He's famously single which makes him a juicy target for paparazzi. The price of a photo of him in a romantic situation with anyone must sell for a fortune."

"That would explain all this security. I guess our only chance to get in touch with him would be to write to his agent, like the website says." Alice sighed.

"We have other options," Paolo assured her. "Let's go."

Giuseppe, who worked at Camillo's Café in the village square, used to play football with Luigi Felice and knew Paolo and his family, Paolo explained, so if he was still in touch with Luigi, he could vouch for them.

By the time she and Paolo got to the café, they were in dire need of replenishing fluid levels so they ordered two coffee granitas and two lemonades with plenty of ice.

The café was quiet so Giuseppe served them and sat at their table.

"So, who have we got here? I've heard rumours," Giuseppe said in tentative English, flicking his towel over his shoulder and grinning at Alice in a friendly way.

"My girlfriend," Paolo replied, taking her hand and intertwining his fingers with hers.

A tingle of electricity ran up Alice's arm. How many more instances of physical contact could she take before she completely forgot that their relationship was only a pretence?

One day she might just get confused and kiss him or hug him when there was no one looking. Then Paolo would know that, for her, it wasn't a pretence anymore. How would she explain herself?

No, she could never tell him that she had feelings for him. He had made it clear that, after what had happened with Rosaria, he wasn't going to embark into romance and love ever again.

All she could do was squeeze his hand back and smile at Giuseppe.

***

Paolo hadn't needed to hold Alice's hand to convince Giuseppe that they were a couple but any excuse was good to have her a little closer.

How was he going to cope when they were back in London and their fake relationship was over?

Once she had made contact with her biological parents she wouldn't need him anymore. Maybe they would never see each other again. The thought gave him an unpleasant shiver.

"What a lovely young lady! You're a lucky man," Giuseppe said, slapping his back.

"I know," Paolo agreed. "Listen, we have a favour to ask you. Do you still play football with Luigi Felice?"

Giuseppe looked at Alice. "So you're a fan of Altavicia's own music star! I'm sorry, I don't play with the lads these days." He turned to Paolo again. "It's funny you ask me because Francesco is a good friend of Luigi. You should go to him."

It was as if a boulder had landed on Paolo's shoulders. Francesco was Rosaria's older brother. Paolo had thought about asking him, certainly, but it wasn't that simple. Francesco had never liked him and Paolo reciprocated the feeling. Rosaria's brother was Luigi Felice's age, much older than Paolo, and he had always treated Paolo with contempt and undisguised annoyance.

Paolo would rather have a tooth pulled out without anaesthetic than ask this guy a favour! In addition, he didn't have Francesco's number so he would have to ask Rosaria for help, something else he didn't desire.

"Who's Francesco?" Alice asked, eager-eyed.

"Rosaria's brother."

"Oh." Alice frowned.

Why was she looking so sad? She couldn't know how much asking Rosaria would cost him nor that his relationship with her brother was fraught. Hadn't the two women hit it off from the first night? Alice should be happy that their chances hung on Rosaria!

"I'll ask her," she offered. "Meeting

Luigi is my problem, not yours."

Technically that might be true, but Paolo cared so much about her that her problems were now his.

"Don't worry. I will."

"I insist. It's my duty," she said with uncharacteristic petulance.

What was going on? He had a feeling that Alice didn't like the idea of him talking to Rosaria. He might have said that she was jealous but that was impossible. Alice didn't care about him in that way.

"Shall I bring you some more lemonade?" Giuseppe asked sheepishly.

"No, thanks, we're fine. We should get going," Paolo said.

"Yes, let's go" Alice agreed tersely.

CHAPTER 31

They walked home in silence. Alice's cheeks were flushed by the heat and she was walking slower than on the way there. He shouldn't have had her walk all this way but it might offend her if he offered to go collect the Vespa to pick her up.

"Is Rosaria coming to dinner tonight?" she asked just before they got home.

"I'm not sure. I'll ring her about Luigi Felice as soon as we get home."

"So you still have her number." Her accusing tone took him aback.

"Of course. She's my sister-in-law-to-be," he said defensively. "If I delete her number, I'll be accused of being unforgiving. If I keep her number, I'm guilty of still holding a candle for her. How can I satisfy you?"

"You don't have to worry about satisfying me. What I think doesn't matter."

She was wrong. What she thought mattered a lot but he could never tell her. "I'll talk to Rosaria." He smiled to lighten the mood. "I don't want you two getting together and talking behind my back about what a lousy boyfriend I was."

They had got to the gate of the house and he was about to push it open for her but she didn't walk through.

Instead, she looked at him, curious. "Were you a lousy boyfriend?"

"I must have been or Rosaria wouldn't have switched over to Marcello."

He wanted to get into the house and put an end to the conversation but Alice stood across the gate, blocking his way.

"Is that what you think? That Rosaria left you because you weren't a good boyfriend?" she challenged.

He raised his palms in the air. "Is that wrong?"

"Rosaria leaving you for your brother has nothing to do with the experience she had with you. You could have been the most fantastic, perfect boyfriend and fiancé but, if she had fallen in love with someone else, it wouldn't have made any difference. Paolo, what happened with Rosaria is nothing to do with you."

"How can it not be if she left me?"

She shook her head. "You're being pig-headed and self-centred. Not everything is about you. Rosaria fell in love with your brother while she wasn't in love with you. The actions were all hers, can't you see?"

"I see it as a woman going into a shoe shop and choosing one pair of shoes instead of another. Are you saying it's nothing to do with the pair of shoes but the woman?"

"Yes! The woman's feet didn't fit the first pair of shoes."

"No: the shoes were too small. There was something wrong with the shoes," he insisted.

"Paolo, the shoes were the right size for another woman, just not for her."

Alice sounded a little exasperated. Why did she care about what he thought?

"Anyway, boyfriends are not shoes for women to walk on—or over!" she said.

"Okay, that was a bad metaphor," he admitted.

"Even if Rosaria told me what a lousy boyfriend you were to her, it wouldn't make any difference to me," she said quietly, avoiding his gaze.

No doubt she meant that she wasn't interested because she would never want him as her boyfriend anyway.

He forced a smile. "Quite."

Finally, she walked through the gate and Paolo followed her in.

CHAPTER 32

That evening, Rosaria joined the family for dinner. Paolo waited until she was sitting on her own on the bench by the orange grove, smoking a cigarette. He took a glass of red wine for liquid courage and walked over.

"Mind if I join you?"

"Oh, hello. Not at all," she said, gathering her dress to make space for him on the bench.

They sat in silence for a while, he nursing his wine glass and she smoking her cigarette, both watching the waxy leaves of the orange trees sway gently in the evening breeze.

Since their break-up, he had been cold and standoffish with her, so asking her for a favour was a little awkward.

"I've got to know Alice more now and I still believe that she's a lovely girl. But I'm sure you know that already," Rosaria said.

"I do."

"Yet you're still holding back. Why?"

This wasn't the conversation he had planned. He took a gulp of his wine. "I don't know what you're talking about."

"Your body language with each other. I can't quite put my finger on it but there's something amiss."

He knew what was amiss: the millions of kisses he was holding back; the embraces he had to refrain from; the caresses he wanted to give but couldn't justify.

"We're just fine," he said with cold finality and drained his glass.

"Sorry, I shouldn't be sticking my nose into your affairs. But it would be a great shame if you kept her at a distance. She clearly loves you."

Paolo almost spat his wine over his shorts. "What makes you think that?"

"Why are you so surprised that your girlfriend loves you? Actually, no, don't answer."

"I wasn't going to."

"Yes, you were. You were going to say some barb about me." She raised a knowing eyebrow.

"I'm over all that."

"May be, but you still haven't forgiven me. I can tell. I don't blame you, so we're not going to talk about me, but Alice. The poor girl is smitten and you are keeping her at arms' length. Please, don't let what I've done to you stop you loving someone else. If that happens, I won't be able to forgive myself either. But clearly this isn't the conversation you were planning to have when you sat down on this bench. What did you want to talk about?"

There was no point pretending that he had sat next to her just to admire the orange grove.

"I wanted to ask you a favour. It's actually for Alice."

Rosaria smiled. "I'm glad it is. Then you do care."

He sure did but there was nothing to be glad about. His situation with Alice was a mess. "She'd like to meet Luigi Felice. As your brother is a friend of his, do you think he could arrange a private meeting for Alice?"

"A meeting, yes. Private, I'm not sure. Why does it have to be private?"

He couldn't tell Rosaria about Alice's relationship with Luigi. He had no right to drop a bombshell like that. "That's okay. Any meeting will do."

"I'll talk to Francesco. I'm sure that something can be arranged."

"Make sure to tell him it's for Alice, not for me."

Rosaria smiled. "Francesco doesn't hate you, Paolo. He's just very protective of me. He's now giving the cold shoulder to Marcello, would you believe? I think he'll wear mourning clothes at our wedding." She chuckled.

"You could have told me years ago that it wasn't personal," Paolo growled. "I wouldn't have been looking behind my back all the time I was in your house, in fear he might be lurking under the stairs with murderous intentions!"

She chuckled. "I thought you had worked it out. Anyway, you were right to be on the alert: he probably had murderous intentions." She put her cigarette down and turned serious. "I'm glad you've done this for Alice."

"What have I done?"

"Forced yourself to come and talk to me. I'm sure you must have dreaded this conversation, especially if you thought that Francesco was after your blood. Off you go, now: I won't keep you squirming here any longer. I'll text you the time and place where you can take Alice to meet Luigi."

CHAPTER 33

Paolo sat on the step of his artist's hut and looked out to the sea. The view was spectacular—green mountains, turquoise sea and blue sky streaked with white wisps of clouds.

All the ingredients to move the heart and inspire a piece of art were present but, instead of inspiration for his sculpture, all he could think of was Alice.

He knew that she hadn't gone to the market with his mum and sisters today because she loved shopping but had done it to give him time and space to work on his sculpture.

She couldn't know that he could take all the space and time he wanted but she would still follow him around in his heart and thoughts.

Maybe he needed an enclosed space instead of this open view, to contain his thoughts and focus his mind.

He got up and went inside his hut which had once been a shack where shepherds found shelter in bad weather. Paolo paid a rent to the shepherds and had repaired the cracks, secured the windows and door and filled the place with his art materials.

The shepherds still had a key to it to use if necessary and it had never happened that Paolo had found himself there in bad weather, so they had not trodden on each other's toes.

He wouldn't be able to carve marble inside but he could sketch and make clay models of the sculptures he would then carve in London.

Before that, most important of all,

he had to get inspiration.

It was here that he had conceived those pieces that Gus had admired. They had been heart-rending sculptures about romantic love. Paolo had believed he was in love with Rosaria but now he realised he had been in love with love.

Back then, he had been overflowing with happiness and optimism. Now he was jaded. He couldn't add a new piece to that collection or even recreate the same sculptures. How could he create a completely new work of art about love?

Here, high on the mountains, he had always felt able to soar, but not today. He turned his phone on and checked the time. Time to take Alice to meet Luigi Felice.

CHAPTER 34

Alice and Paolo sat on the bench by the football fields. They had come early so they wouldn't miss Luigi at the end of the game.

Every Wednesday, when he was in Altavicia, Luigi Felice played five-a-side football with his old pals. One of them was Rosaria's brother.

Francesco had mentioned to Luigi that a fan wanted to meet him and the tenor had agreed to greet her briefly after the game.

As she watched the game from the other side of the green metal netting, Alice rehearsed what she was going to say. As she couldn't tell Luigi her real reason in company, her goal today was to secure another, private, meeting. Paolo had helped her translate her speech into Italian.

"Which one is he?" she asked Paolo. All the players looked similar.

"The one who's just got the ball."

He was running after the ball like any other man. He seemed so ordinary.

"Are you okay?" Paolo asked, taking her hand in his and squeezing it.

"A little nervous, of course, but I'm as ready as could be. Did you get some work done up in your hut?"

He winced and she immediately wished she hadn't asked. "Sorry, it's none of my business."

"I'm finding it hard to create this piece," he confessed. "I'm struggling. I haven't told anyone so please keep it to yourself."

"Of course. Why do you think it's so hard? Have I distracted you with all my drama?" She felt so guilty.

"No, I've been struggling for a while. I hoped that coming here would unlock the Muse but it hasn't."

"Can I help in any way? Do you need a model? I don't mean I'm model material but if you need a real-type model..." she felt her cheeks redden, "well, you know what I mean."

He smiled. "Thanks, that's very kind. I'd love to take up your offer but I couldn't justify it. You see, I have absolutely no idea what this sculpture will be. I don't even know if it's going to be a human form or something else. I've never been in this situation before and honestly, Alice, I'm scared."

"What's this sculpture about? If you're allowed to say."

"It's to be a wedding present. It's about romantic love." He sighed.

"The way you say it, it could have been a sculpture for mausoleum!"

"That's the problem: the theme

for this sculpture doesn't work for me. I don't believe in romantic love anymore."

His words hit her like a landslide. She had been wrong to think that he might have feelings for her. Nothing had changed since he had told her on the aeroplane that he was done with relationship and love.

All his delicate attentions, all the little signs that she had interpreted as affection, had been misread by her. They had been as fake as the ruse for his family.

She felt deflated and then angry with herself for feeling that way.

***

"Ciao!" a voice boomed at her side. Unmistakeably a tenor's voice.

Alice whipped around. "Ciao," she replied.

In front of her was her biological father, smiling obliviously.

"I hear you are a fan from England,"

he said in English. "I think I can guess which is your favourite song of mine."

He hummed a tune and it was clear that Alice was supposed to recognise it.

"The lovely shores of England, chalky white and green as can be," Paolo sang in Italian, coming to her rescue.

"Oh, yes, I love that song!" Alice lied.

Luigi smiled. "I thought so. Are you coming to Wimbledon?"

Alice blanked. What had tennis to do with it?

Paolo rescued her again. "We couldn't get tickets for your concert but a friend has promised to give us some."

So Luigi meant Wimbledon Concert Hall! Alice wished a crater could open in the ground and suck her down to the roots of Etna.

This meeting was going horribly

wrong. At any moment, Luigi would find out that she wasn't a real fan and wouldn't give her a second chance.

"I'm not one of your fans," she blurted out loudly.

Francesco and all the other players stopped towelling their necks, pulling off their T-shirts and changing their shoes. Silence dropped like a bomb.

"I was sent to you by Simona," Alice confessed.

"Simona?" Luigi cocked his head.

"Simona Latta."

Recognition washed over Luigi's face like a tsunami. He let out a long, slow breath. "How is she?" he asked tentatively as if he wasn't sure whether he wanted to know the answer.

"She's well."

Relief skittered across his eyes. "Is she here?" He looked around, suddenly more alert.

"No, she's in Reggio Calabria."

"Why has she sent you to me? Who are you?"

Alice swallowed. Could she say it? "I'm her daughter. I'm twenty-seven," she murmured.

Alice could almost see the neurons firing in his head at the speed of electricity, the pieces of the puzzle coming together and realization sinking.

Luigi's eyes widened, his mouth dropped and his hand went to Alice's cheek. He touched her gently, gingerly, as if to convince himself that she was real and not a dream.

He scanned her face, perhaps recognising himself or Simona in every feature.

As he was taking her all in, Alice was too. Luigi was a mixture of familiar and strange.

"You've got to tell me more." He glanced quickly over his shoulders. "But not here. Will you come to my house?"

"Yes."

She took Paolo's hand to show that she wasn't going anywhere without him.

"Do you know where I live?" Luigi asked him.

"Of course."

"Then let me go ahead and follow me in five minutes, will you?"

"Sure."

They watched him say goodbye to his friends, get into his car—an ordinary hatchback— and drive off.

"I must thank Francesco before we go," Paolo told her.

"Yes, me, too."

"No problem at all." Francesco slapped Paolo's back when they joined him. "I hope Alice got the autograph she wanted."

"Thanks. If there's anything I can ever do for you, let me know."

"Same for me," Alice said in Italian.

Francesco's eyes widened. "I thought you didn't speak Italian."

"I've learnt a bit while staying here."

"You've learnt a lot, well done!" He turned to Paolo again. "There is something you could do for me. Keep an eye on your brother and make sure he treats my sister as good as you did."

Paolo was speechless for a moment, then he nodded. "I will."

They got on Paolo's Vespa and rode to Luigi's villa.

"I hope Luigi was all right driving. He seemed quite shaken," Alice said.

"I hope so, too. If anything happened to him, his real fans would stab you with their autograph pens. On that topic, I can't believe that you didn't think of bringing a pen and a notebook for an autograph. If you were trying to pass yourself as a fan, you did a very poor job!"

She laughed. How could she have imagined doing this trip without

Paolo?

It wasn't just his translations and his local connections that she would have missed but so much more. He always knew how to make her feel better. Whether she needed encouragement, comfort, advice or reining in, he was there.

He had been a true companion for her. Yet he would never be anything more.

CHAPTER 35

They rang the intercom and, this time, the gate opened at once. A short drive flanked by cordons of red pelargonium ran up to the villa. The façade had a rustic and old-fashioned look to it with wide, low arches decorated with traditional maiolica tiles.

Luigi had changed into shorts and T-shirt. His hair was wet as if he'd had a shower.

"Let's sit on the terrace," he said, still studying Alice with a mixture of wonder and shock.

He led them to some comfy chairs on a secluded terrace at the back of the villa.

"What would you like to drink, er...?"

"Paolo."

"Alice. My name is Alice," she told him.

"Alice," Luigi whispered to himself.

"Nothing for me," Paolo said.

"Not for me, either."

"I need a stiff drink!" Luigi went behind a little bar and poured himself a whisky.

"How is Simona?" he asked as he sat down with them.

"She's well," Alice replied.

"What has she told you about me?"

"That you two were in love, she was expecting your baby and you planned to elope but, when her parents found out, they locked her in her room. The next thing she knew, you and your family had moved to Rome."

He winced at the painful memory. "Do I need to ask if she was able to keep the baby?"

"You have her in front of you," Alice confirmed.

Tears bobbed into his eyes. He leaped from his chair and pulled her into a hug. "Thank heavens!"

"Why didn't you contact Simona?" Alice asked, trying not to sound accusing.

He sighed. "I did but my letters were marked 'return to sender'. I thought it might be her parents' doing so I kept writing to her until the letters came back with 'recipient not known at this address'. At that point, I realised her family had moved and I lost all hope. I worked hard at the music conservatoire in the hope that, once I became famous, she would know how to find me. Every time I gave a concert I hoped she'd turn up backstage, asking for me. But it never happened."

"You could have searched for her online," Alice argued. "That's how I found her."

"I had no access to the internet back then. When it became possible to search, so much time had passed that I was sure she had moved on. If she had a husband and a family, I didn't want to know. Wait. What do you mean, you 'found' her?"

"Simona had to give me away for adoption and I was brought up in England."

"I hope your adoptive parents were kind. Please, thank them for me."

"I can't. They've passed away."

"I'm so sorry. Then, when you see Simona, thank her. I know she must have fought against her parents to bring you to life."

Alice's throat knotted. He still loved Simona! This man, who could have scores of girlfriends thanks to his wealth and fame, hadn't forgotten his first love. His only love. "Why don't you thank her yourself? I believe she'd like it very much if you got in touch. By the way, she's single like you."

Luigi frowned. "Maybe the past is best left in the past."

"I don't think so or I wouldn't be here."

Luigi asked questions about Alice's childhood, her parents and her life. "And you found love." He smiled at Paolo.

It was true, she had fallen in love. She just wasn't ever going to be loved back. She nodded and smiled, knowing she mustn't show the sadness in her heart.

CHAPTER 36

By the time they left Luigi Felice's villa, it was already dark and well past dinnertime. Paolo had rung his mother to tell her not to wait for them for dinner and had explained that they were having a meeting with the tenor.

Lia never liked it when someone was late or skipped one of her meals but she had reacted unusually well. Paolo put it down to her being a staunch fan.

He was a little surprised, therefore, when he and Alice returned home to find his mother waiting for them in the front porch with a thunderous expression.

"Oh, dear. Didn't you warn your mum that we were going to miss dinner?" Alice whispered when they removed their helmets.

"I did and I thought she had been fine about it."

They got off the Vespa at the same time as his mother stood up and planted her fists on her hips. There was no mistaking that she was cross.

Paolo rocked the Vespa up onto its stand and raised his hands in innocence. "I thought you knew, Mamma."

"I didn't," she spat.

"But I told you."

"All you told me were lies!"

"What are you talking about?"

He had been in trouble with his mother plenty of times but he usually knew why.

"You and Alice. Why did you lie to me?" she shouted.

His first reaction was the

indignation of someone who has been falsely accused. Alice had become so much a part of him, was so entrenched in his heart that, for a moment, he couldn't get what his mother was cross about.

That was until he remembered that Alice wasn't actually his girlfriend and their relationship had been only a ruse.

Vittoria must have told their mother. She had warned him she would do it.

"What is your mother saying?" Alice asked, alarmed.

"I'll tell you later." He could only cope with one disaster at a time.

His mother gave them both such a wounded glance that it cut right inside his heart.

"Don't blame her, Mamma. She's been dragged into this by me. She didn't want to do it."

"You should have listened to her! Why did you think to trick me like this?"

"You wanted me to have a girlfriend. It made you happy."

"But now I'm more unhappy than before."

"What is she saying?" Alice demanded, pulling his arm.

"Why did you let it go on for so long? I've grown attached to Alice and now I feel, well, bereft!" his mum pressed on.

"You would have grown attached to a real girlfriend, too, and you would have been sad when we broke up. Most relationships end," he said defensively.

"No, Paolo. I wouldn't have grown attached to any girl. Alice is special. If you really wanted to pull this trick on me, you should have chosen a different girl." Lia sounded tired, bitter and disappointed. She turned around and went into the house, leaving Paolo and Alice alone.

He stared at the empty threshold

after his mother had disappeared. He didn't know what to say to her or to Alice.

The evening dew felt like tears, the cicadas' songs sounded like dirges and the stars in the sky were judging eyes.

"She has found out the truth about us, hasn't she?" Alice asked bitterly.

Paolo wasn't sure what the truth about them was. "Yes, I'm afraid she has." He shook his head. "Go on, tell me that you knew it, that you warned me and that I refused to listen. It's all true."

"It's not all about you or me, Paolo, it's about the people we've hurt. Everyone has been hurt," she said, then muttered to herself, "including us."

She climbed the steps into the house, leaving him outside alone with the cicadas and the stars.

He squatted and held his head in his hands. He had hurt the two women he loved most.

Yes, he loved Alice. He couldn't keep running away from this truth.

From the darkness of the place where he was squatting, the stars seemed to shine more brightly. He had needed to sink low to be able to see them more clearly.

It was the same with the heart. He could see clearly that he loved Alice. And that he had to tell her.

CHAPTER 37

Paolo straightened up and marched into the house armed with courage and resolution. He knocked on Alice's door.

"Go away," she replied quietly from the inside.

"Can we talk?"

"We've talked enough."

"Please."

The door opened a crack.

"What is it?"

Her eyes were red and her cheeks wet. It broke his heart to see it and to know that he had caused it.

"I'm so sorry."

"Too late."

"I love you, Alice."

"We've told enough lies. Let's stop."

"It's not a lie!"

"You thought that lying to your mother would make her happier. My parents thought that lying to me would make me happier. But lies come out eventually, and they hurt. Go away, Paolo, please."

She began closing the door and he didn't stop her. What would be the point? He could demand that she listen but he couldn't force her to believe him.

When the door clicked shut, he stormed into his room and packed an overnight bag and art supplies. The only place where he could spend tonight was his hut. As far as possible from the woman he could never have.

First he had to apologise to his mum, though. He grabbed his satchel and went to the terrace, where he found her listening to her portable radio.

He knelt next to her so that they were at eye-level and took her hands. "I'm sorry, Mamma, I messed up. I shouldn't have lied to you or asked Alice to lie."

"It's my fault, Paolo. I wanted so much for you to be happy that I believed what I wanted to be true. When you told me that you were coming home with a friend, I didn't believe she was just a friend. You tried to tell me a few times but I insisted that it wasn't true."

"I should have stuck with the truth," he said.

"We all make mistakes. The important thing is to forgive others as we'd want to be forgiven." She tried to hug him but his satchel came between them. "What's this? Are you going out?"

"I'm going to work at the hut."

"Can't you go in the morning?"

"I can't. Look after Alice for me."

"When are you coming back?"

"Tomorrow morning."

"Have you told her?"

"No. It's not a good time to talk to her. I should be back before she's up anyway."

His mother cupped his face and kissed his forehead. "I'm not going to tell anyone that you and Alice are not together because I think you should be. I hope you two see sense and turn your pretence into the real thing."

"It might be too late."

"It's never too late. There is a remedy to everything other than death."

"I hope so."

He kissed her cheek and left.

Riding in the night was refreshing. The sound of the engine revving up the hill as he dropped the gears reminded him of his own heart labouring under the strain of love. Love was a mountain to climb. He hadn't realised that he'd started climbing it the moment he got onto the plane with Alice.

He remembered her shocked face when he told her that he needed her to pretend to be his girlfriend. Her blush when they kissed in front of all his family. The times he had held her hand; the tears he had wiped from her face. Would he have shirked away from all that if he had known he would have fallen in love?

No. He would have changed only one thing: the lie he had told his family. Before telling anyone, he should have fought to make it come true.

He parked under the carob tree and killed the engine. The cicadas welcomed him with a jaunty song and the breeze brought up to him the sounds of the sea.

Now that he had let love loose in his heart, the hut felt like home again.

He turned off his phone, turned on the solar-powered torch and started sketching. Ideas poured out of his fingers and onto the paper.

A mountain took shape through his charcoal pencil. Yes, love was a mountain. Struggle, pain and reward. Danger. Precipices from which there was no stepping back. Views and height. Springs of pure water.

Attracted by his torch—the only light on that mountain—moths flocked to him on their elegant velvety wings, first spectators of his new creation.

CHAPTER 38

Alice waited until she couldn't hear the rumble of Paolo's Vespa any longer, then she ventured out of her room to look for Lia. She owed the woman an apology and the truth about her real reasons for this trip.

Alice walked onto terrace so softly that Lia only noticed her when she sat down on the deckchair next to hers.

"Ciao," Lia said with a smile which Alice felt she didn't deserve.

"I'm sorry I've lied to you," she told her.

"I played a part, too. Paolo said he was coming with a friend but I didn't believe him. I insisted that you must be his girlfriend until he gave in and agreed. He lied to me to keep me happy. I'm sorry he asked you to play along with it. But tell me, why did you agree to play along? What was in it for you?"

Alice swallowed. Her reason for agreeing had changed over time and both the original and the new one were difficult to admit.

"At first, Paolo and I had a deal: if I played the part of his girlfriend, he would help me find my birth mother in Reggio. We called the deal, 'a mother for a mother'. But then, playing girlfriend started feeling natural. I..."

"You fell in love with my son."

Tears bobbed in Alice's eyes. "It wasn't meant to happen."

Lia hugged her. She smelled of delicious food and also a bit like Paolo —the man Alice loved but who would never love her back.

STEFANIA HARTLEY

***

Paolo worked until the first glow of dawn peeped over the tops of the Aspromonte mountains. Satisfied with his sketch for the sculpture, he started work on a clay model.

He didn't feel sleepy, tired or hungry. He was in a creative fever.

It wasn't the desperation of an approaching deadline but a joyous creative urgency. He had fallen in love with Alice and was falling in love with life all over again.

Yes, she had rejected him, but she had been cross with him about the ruse. He would try again. He would invite her up here, where no family, friend or girlfriend had ever been allowed, and he would open his heart to her.

CHAPTER 39

The rattle and rumble of a motorbike engine brought him back to earth. Paolo put down the clay he was holding and looked down on the road that snaked up the mountain and led to the hut.

It was his brother on his motorbike with Rosaria riding pillion!

He had never told anyone the location of his hut. Marcello and Rosaria must have asked the shepherds. This visit must be due to something serious.

He covered the clay model with a damp cloth to keep it from drying out and rushed down the steep footpath.

His brother parked his flaming-red Ducati under the carob tree next to Paolo's Vespa. He and Rosaria dismounted, neither making eye contact with him.

"What's the matter?"

"We'd like a word," Marcello said.

Paolo led them up to the steps in front of the hut—the only place he could offer them to sit down.

Marcello rested his elbows on his knees and steepled his hands. "Mamma has confessed she put pressure on you to come to our wedding. She told me that you didn't want to come."

"It's true," Paolo replied candidly. He'd had enough of subterfuges. They always ended up in a mess.

"That came as a surprise. I had thought that things were settled between us but I should have guessed that certain actions can't be forgiven so easily. You and I have never had a serious conversation about what happened. It might help clear the air between us," Marcello suggested nervously.

"You and I have never talked seriously about anything," Paolo flung back. They had always joked, teased and mocked each other but had never had serious exchanges. "I guess it's time to grow up." Paolo meant this mostly about himself but Marcello nodded and hung his head as if he had been chastised. Why was it so hard for the two of them to communicate?

"When you and Rosaria were together," Marcello began, "I had feelings for her but I tried to squash them. I didn't want to fall for my brother's girlfriend. I avoided being at home when you two were there and I tried to keep away from her. Sometimes I was even rude. You ticked me off a few times, remember?"

Paolo nodded.

"Seeing you together was agony, but when I started noticing that you two were growing apart, I felt hopeful even though I hated myself for it. Sometimes I thought that Rosaria was looking at me in a different way than before but then I'd convince myself that I had just imagined what I wished to be true. I tried so hard to stamp my feelings out once I suspected that Rosaria felt the same about me. I decided that it would be wrong."

Rosaria cleared her voice. "I have a part in this, too, Paolo. When you and I started going out, we were only kids. We had met at school and that was all we knew of each other. As we grew up and got to know each other better, it became clear to me that our goals and dreams were incompatible. Of course, I had grown to know your family very well, including Marcello. His plans for the future seemed more aligned with

THE ITALIAN FAKE DATE

mine, while your dreams of moving to London scared me. If I had followed you there, I would always have been homesick and resentful towards you. If we had stayed here, you would always have resented me. When you gave up your dream and decided to stay in Altavicia and get married to me, I panicked. We would never have been happy together and I had already started falling in love with Marcello."

Paolo looked out to the sea. "You are right. It would never have worked. We were hurtling towards marriage out of inertia. We had got together as teens and had kept going without questioning whether we were suited to each other. Or were actually in love." He looked at her. "I must thank you for what you've done. Your bravery has saved us both."

She let out a breath and smiled. "I wasn't expecting gratitude. Forgiveness would have been enough."

"You have that, too."

Paolo looked Marcello in the eyes. "I'm sorry for what you've been through. I didn't realise."

"Well, that was the idea. Can you forgive me, Paolo?"

"There's nothing to forgive."

Paolo pulled his brother upright and hugged him. They hadn't hugged each other for years and it felt like coming home.

"Shouldn't you be getting ready to go to the airport, Paolo?" Rosaria asked.

"Airport? Why?"

"We rushed here to talk to you because we thought you were leaving with Alice."

"Alice is leaving?"

"She was packing and saying goodbye to everyone at home," Marcello said. "I told her I'd been hoping she could come to our wedding but she said she had to go home."

"We thought you had decided to skip our wedding so we came here to ask for your forgiveness," Rosaria added.

Paolo felt as if an entire mountain of marble had landed on him. "I shouldn't have turned off my phone! What time is it?"

"Almost midday."

He had meant to be back home before Alice had got up to apologise to her again. Instead, he had disappeared without a word. No wonder she was going home!

CHAPTER 40

He ran down the footpath and jumped on his Vespa but Marcello ran after him. "I'll give you a lift. We'll be faster."

The Ducati was easily faster than the Vespa, especially in Marcello's hands.

"I'll close the hut and ride your Vespa back," Rosaria shouted after them.

Marcello tackled the mountain's hairpin bends so fast that their knees skimmed the tarmac. It didn't stop Paolo turning on his phone and checking it. No calls or messages from Alice.

He rang her but the call went straight to answering machine. Was she already on the plane or just ignoring his calls? He couldn't let her go home without speaking to her. He rang his mother.

"Has Alice left?"

"Where are you? I almost asked your brother to go and fetch you but that would have meant telling him the truth about you and Alice, which is not my place to tell."

"Please, Mamma, answer me: is Alice still a home?"

"Yes and no."

Paolo felt like howling with frustration. This wasn't the time for his mother to be talking in riddles. "What do you mean?"

"She's called a taxi. Your father offered to drive her but she refused."

"Don't let her get into the taxi, please! Delay her until we get there."

"I won't be able to hold her for long.

The taxi will be here any moment." Through the phone came the honk of a car horn. "Oh, dear, it's already here."

"Do anything you can to hold her up."

"For how long?"

Paolo looked ahead. They were still halfway up the mountain. "A couple of minutes."

"I'll try."

Paolo pocketed his phone.

"Technically, we're not a couple of minutes away," Marcello called behind him.

Paolo had shouted so loud that is brother must have heard the whole conversation.

"Can you make it happen?"

"Sure. Tuck you elbows in, bro!"

For the next hairpin bends Paolo was glad he had on a long-sleeved top. It wasn't just his elbows that saw the tarmac close up, he suspected his shoulders did, too!

Whenever they met another vehicle on a single-track road, the Ducati roadster took to the verges as if it was a scrambler bike.

Even so, when they skidded to a halt in front of the gate of their parents' home, they found that they had diced with death for nothing. There was no taxi. Paolo was too late.

CHAPTER 41

"We'll race the taxi," Marcello suggested. He never needed the slightest excuse for any kind of racing.

"Let's ask Mamma for more news first." Paolo vaulted the bike and ran indoors, where he stopped.

His mother was lying on the sofa beneath a blanket, being hovered over solicitously by his father, his sisters and... Alice.

He didn't know whether to be relieved that Alice was still there or concerned that his mother was clearly unwell.

"Alice! Mamma!"

Suddenly, Lia opened her eyes. "Here you are, you silly boy!"

She pulled back the blanket and sat up upright. "I'm all better. Sorry about that," she said to her family.

"What's going on?" Alice asked, looking with confusion from mother to son and back.

Lia was arguing with her husband who seemed intent on calling an ambulance.

"I asked my mother to delay you until I got here. I guess she resorted to desperate measures. Please, don't go, Alice. I know I don't deserve you and I never meant for this to happen but, well, I've fallen in love with you."

"How can I believe you? You've lied to so many people!" Alice cried.

"The only person who has lied today is me," Lia pointed out.

"You scared us half to death!" his father scolded her.

"Plus you nearly wasted emergency

services' time," one of his sisters said.

"Sorry," she said sheepishly.

Alice looked at Paolo. "You told everyone that I was your girlfriend, not just your family but everyone we met. You even told Simona and Luigi when there was no need to lie to them at all. Lying seems to come so easily to you."

"Wait, aren't you two boyfriend and girlfriend?" his father asked, confused.

Vittoria gave Paolo a look that said, "I told you so".

He took Alice's hands in his and she didn't pull them away.

"It started as a white lie but quickly turned into a wish. That's why I told everyone: I wanted it to become reality. I love you, Alice."

"You told me that you don't believe in love anymore."

"I do now."

Rosaria burst in through the door. "Did you make it in time?" she asked breathlessly, then smiled when she saw Alice and Paolo holding hands.

Alice looked questioningly at him.

"I've had to ask for help from many people to reach you before you left," Paolo explained.

Marcello stepped into the room. "We did some pretty dangerous riding," he added with a wicked grin.

"Mamma mia, I'm going to faint for real now!" their mother said.

"No more fainting from you," Agostino said sternly.

"Where have you been?" Alice asked.

Paolo still had no idea whether she had forgiven him or was ever going to, let alone love him back. But if she wanted time to decide what she really felt, that was only fair. "I'll show you. Come," he invited her.

"You'll need these, then!" Rosaria threw the Vespa's keys at him and winked.

CHAPTER 42

Riding on Paolo's Vespa with her arms around him, Alice felt at home. Yet she couldn't help recalling that, last night, he had left without telling her anything.

She had imagined him asleep in the bedroom next to hers while he was miles away on top of a mountain. Could she ever trust him?

They parked under a tree with long, dangly brown pods and climbed a footpath leading to a hut.

"This is my workshop," he told her proudly. "I've never shown it to anyone and none of my family knows its location. This morning, Marcello and Rosaria had to ask the shepherd I rent it from or they wouldn't have found it. I'm glad they did."

"Why did you disappear like that?"

"I was sure you didn't want to talk to me, and I had planned to return before you woke up. Then, inspiration struck and I lost the sense of time. Next thing I knew it was late morning and Marcello and Rosaria were here. Come in," he said, opening the door.

She stepped inside. His artist's hut was small but beautiful. Tools, pens and pencils were all lined up tidily on the shelves. Pictures of sculptures and paintings were pinned with thumbtacks to the wooden walls. A milk pail filled with water sat in a corner next to a block of clay wrapped in transparent plastic. And in the centre of the tiny room was a wooden pedestal covered with a cloth.

Paolo stood in a corner, watching

her.

"Why are you smiling?" she asked.

"Because you look like you belong here. You're the missing piece."

"Do you mean you needed a model?" she questioned cynically.

"No, not that."

She thought she understood what he meant but she wasn't ready to let him off the hook quite yet. "What's under the cloth?"

"A clay model of my sculpture."

"I'm glad you found your inspiration." She meant it.

"It's thanks to you."

"I didn't do anything."

"You made me fall in love again."

Her heart galloped in her chest but her head was still swimming with warnings. "May I see or is it a secret?"

"It's not a secret for you."

He lifted the drape. It was an embracing couple forming an upward spiral, reminiscent of a mountain.

Alice stepped closer. "It's beautiful."

"This is only a scale model. It'll be a lot bigger," Paolo explained.

"It reminds me of another sculpture I've seen in art books," she mused.

"This, perhaps?" He pointed to a picture on the wall of a marble couple embracing and kissing.

"Yes, that's the one!"

"'The Kiss' by Rodin. Its original name was actually 'Francesca da Rimini'."

She liked that. Francesca was the name Simona had given her when she was born. "Who was she?"

"A thirteen-century noblewoman who fell in love with her brother-in-law. All these other pictures have also been inspired by that famous couple." He pointed to printed images that lined the walls. "The famous Italian writer, Dante, wrote about them, too. Unfortunately for them he placed them in hell."

Alice reviewed the pictures. "Why did they inspire so many artists?"

"I guess it's the tragedy of their story. They were both skewered to death by Francesca's husband who caught them *in flagrante*."

Realization dawned on her: there was a parallel between the story of this woman cheating on her husband with his brother and Paolo's own experience. "Is it what inspired you, too? I'm sorry, that was an indelicate question."

"No. And for the record, I do not plan on murdering my brother and Rosaria! We've cleared the air between us and I hold no grudge against them."

"So what did attract you to their story?"

"Francesca's lover is called Paolo." He smiled tenderly. "And you were born Francesca."

She took a deep breath. "What inspired you was you and me?"

"Yes," he replied in a husky voice, stepping closer.

His gaze dropped to her lips and hers to his. He circled her waist, she rested her hands on his shoulders and they kissed.

It was even better than the kiss of her first night in Italy.

When they resurfaced for air, she smiled up at him. "I love you, too."

CHAPTER 43

On her first visit to Luigi's villa, Alice had been so busy dealing with the emotions roiling inside her to pay any attention to anything else.

This time she could appreciate the stunning view of the sea and of the coastline, the villa's beautiful rustic décor and the numerous awards and trophies which lined the shelves.

She and Luigi had decided to keep their relationship private, at least until his PR people had planned how to handle it and Luigi had discussed it with Simona. The harsh limelight of the press would be bound to fall upon her.

Luigi had invited Alice, Paolo and his family, Francesco and his family and a few other local friends to a party here. And Simona.

If the reason for the party was to lessen the awkwardness of meeting Simona, it was probably a good idea, in Alice's opinion.

He was making many people happy, after all, especially Paolo's mum who had brought a stack of CDs and T-shirts for Luigi to sign.

He had obliged and was being a gracious host, but every time the intercom rang, he jumped. Each time the door opened, he whipped round to see who had arrived. Alice knew who he was waiting to see.

When Simona finally appeared, she was wearing a colourful dungaree dress with her curls cascading over her shoulders.

Luigi's expression when he saw her

said everything. Alice almost went to introduce them but, of course, they had known each other well before they had known her.

Simona stepped over the threshold and Luigi moved towards her.

Alice couldn't hear what they said to each other but could tell from their body language that they both wanted to hug each other but didn't dare.

When Simona and Luigi entered the party room, Paolo's family turned to look at them with interest. Alice had been given permission to share with them that the pair were her birth parents.

"I can see the family similarity," Rosaria whispered into Alice's ear.

"Genetic similarity. We're not actually a family," Alice replied with regret.

"I'm sure you will soon be."

"We can't."

"Why?"

"It feels wrong."

Rosaria looked into her eyes. "You are family to us yet we don't even share blood. Does that feel wrong?"

"No."

"Then why should it feel wrong to be family to your birth parents?"

"My adoptive parents didn't want Simona to have contact with me. I already feel I've betrayed them."

"Things have changed. You have grown up and so has your birth mother. It's a pity your parents aren't around to tell you but I'm sure they'd be delighted you've found your birth parents. Have you ever thought they might have changed their mind over the years but, once they'd gone down the path of keeping your adoption secret, they had to stick to it?"

"I guess. Maybe that's why they didn't destroy Simona's letters."

"If I was leaving my daughter an orphan, at whatever age, I'd be happy if she got a new family. Husbands and wives can marry again so can't children 'adopt' new parents? It's a bit topsy-turvy, I know."

Alice smiled.

Rosaria's phone rang in her pocket. She pulled it out and looked at the number. "Do you mind if I answer this?" she asked Alice, apprehension in her eyes.

"Of course not."

Alice couldn't understand all of Rosaria's conversation but she could tell it was about the wedding and it wasn't good news.

When Rosaria ended the call, she sighed deeply and sank into the nearest seat.

"Are you alright?"

"Not really. The venue we hired for the wedding banquet has gone bankrupt!"

"Oh, no!" This was bad, and so close to the wedding, too.

"We're not getting our deposit back. Even if we had the money to spend all over again, we won't find another wedding venue at such short notice."

"I'm so sorry. Could you fit your guests in Lia and Agostino's garden?"

"At a push. But the venue was fully catered so we would still be missing the meals. This is a disaster!" Rosaria's eye filled with tears. "I haven't the heart to tell Marcello."

"I will." Alice handed her a tissue.

Her gaze fell on Simona and Luigi, still talking in a corner of the room, and an idea flashed into her mind. Luigi had the perfect venue and Simona was in the catering business. The memory of the deserted workshop in a deserted street with graffiti bobbed into Alice's head. Simona needed all the custom she could get, and the cakes she had prepared for Alice and Paolo that morning had been delicious. She could make them and might know someone who could do savoury dishes.

"Wait here," she told Rosaria, then went up to Simona and Luigi.

She hated interrupting them but this was important. They turned to her with surprise, as if they had completely forgotten that others were around them.

"I need to ask for your help."

Alice explained Rosaria and Marcello's predicament.

"They can have their party here!" Luigi said, beaming.

"And I can do their cakes and desserts. I know someone who can do the rest of the meals. Leave it with me."

Simona, too, looked radiant with happiness.

"When is the happy event?" Luigi asked.

"Next Saturday. Sorry, it's really short notice."

Simona turned to Luigi. "I think we can do it."

There was a spark in Luigi's eyes when Simona said "we".

"Yes, we can."

CHAPTER 44

Paolo watched Marcello and Rosaria exchange vows at the altar and smiled, sincerely happy for them both. As he had expected, some people in the congregation were sending him furtive glances to check his reaction but he didn't mind: he had nothing to hide.

He was even happier now that he had Alice at his side. Not as a fake girlfriend to stave off other people's commiseration or suspicion, but as a real companion, with him for no other reason than love.

Perhaps, one day, she would be standing by his side at that altar, too.

When the service was over and the bride and the groom walked up the aisle towards the exit, Alice circled Paolo's waist and leant her head on his shoulder. "I owe a lot to this wedding."

"Why so?"

"Without it you would never have asked me to be your fake girlfriend." She looked up at him and gave him that smile which made him melt.

"Also, if Rosaria and Marcello hadn't got together, she might be hogging my place still today," she added.

He loved the possessive way she said it. "It's your place, is it?" he teased, kissing the top of her head.

"Absolutely."

Marcello and Rosaria were ambushed by Vittoria, Agatina and the cousins with handfuls of flower petals and rice.

The bridal couple rode off on Marcello's Ducati in a cloud of white tulle, headed for Luigi's villa.

Luigi had been very kind to offer his home for the wedding party, but it was only when they got there that the extent of his generosity was clear.

The villa had been decked in flowers and wedding-themed ornaments and there were uniformed staff at every corner. Marcello and Rosaria had opted for a standing-up buffet to reduce costs, but Luigi had hired tables and chairs and an army of catering staff so that people who wanted to sit down could be served instead.

Simona emerged from the kitchen in her chef's whites with the usual curl escaping from her hat. She looked as radiant and pretty as her cakes.

Paolo was sure that Luigi had relished hosting her in his kitchen for the past three days—which was all the time she had had to prepare everything.

She hadn't accepted any payment for her work and time, only for the ingredients which, she declared, she would have happily donated if she could afford it.

When the party was coming to an end and everyone had raved about her cakes, Paolo went over to her.

"Thank you for this delicious feast. I don't think Marcello and Rosaria would have had cakes so nice if they had had their contracted caterers."

Simona smiled. "It's been my pleasure."

"Please, let us pay for your work."

He was remembering her empty book of orders, the graffiti on the wall and the nuisance calls. Maybe she was in debt and was being hounded by creditors.

She shook her head. "If you don't want to take it as a gift, consider that it has been marketing for my business. Today I've given away so many business cards that I've run out! I've already picked up a few bookings for the coming months, something I sorely needed."

"How is your business doing?" Paolo ventured.

She looked down and sighed. "Ever since I stood up to the local racketeers and refused to pay their 'protection' money, things have been hard. As well as the usual threats and calls, they retaliated by pressuring my clients to take their business elsewhere."

"I'm sorry."

He now admired this woman even more than before. She was as brave now as she had been at sixteen.

"Please, don't tell Alice: I don't want her to get worried. Though maybe I'm assuming I mean to her more than I do. After all, I gave her away."

"I think you mean a lot to her, Simona. You are the child who fought for her life against the grown-ups who were feeding and clothing you. You were very brave."

Tears filled Simona's eyes. "Thank you."

They both looked at Alice who was dancing with Vittoria, Agatina and the cousins out on the terrace.

"She's a lovely girl," Simona said softly.

Paolo hesitated. He hadn't thought this through but it felt right. "I hope that, soon, I can book you for another wedding."

Simona looked up at him and smiled. "I hope that, too."

CHAPTER 45

"Oh, I really don't want to go back to London tomorrow," Alice protested sadly as she and Paolo walked back to his family home.

They had turned down a lift in the car with Agostino and Lia so that they could spend a little time together just on their own.

"Neither do I."

"I guess that you're going to have your work cut out—excuse the pun—to get the sculpture ready in time for Gus' wedding," she told him.

"Yes, it's going to be very tight, and I'll have to juggle my other job around it, too."

"I won't see you much for the next while, then." She hoped she didn't sound too whiny and needy.

"That's out of the question."

Oh, okay. Of course he didn't have time for her. She pushed away the prick of disappointment. Why had she even asked?

He stopped walking and turned her around to face him. "Listen, Alice. There's something I have to tell you."

She swallowed. This was it, then. He was going to tell her that it had been fun while they were on holiday but now he had to concentrate on his work. It was best that they cool things off between them. Paolo had already sacrificed his artistic ambitions for a woman once and had been burnt. He wasn't going to do it again.

Alice steeled herself for the blow. She must not whinge, whine or make him feel bad about letting her go. This

man had helped her find her birth
parents—he didn't owe her anything.
If she had happened to fall in love and
wanted more from him than he could
give, then that wasn't his fault. "Yes,
Paolo?" she whispered.

He frowned. "I don't think I can..."

She couldn't bear to hear the words.
"I understand. It's okay. Don't feel bad
about it."

"I don't feel bad about it," he said,
surprised.

He didn't feel bad about breaking
up with her? That hurt even more!

"The thing is, I don't think I can last
a single day without being with you."

What was that?

He put one hand on his heart, took
hers with the other and laid it on
his chest. She could feel his heart
thumping.

"I know it's early days and neither of
us have thought this through properly,
the way sensible people would do. But

I've gone the sensible route in the past and it didn't help me see where love was and where it wasn't. This time, I feel that it's right. I want us to be together till death do us part. Alice, will you be my wife?"

Her head swam and her heart soared. She let out a gasp.

"I'm sorry. You deserved better than being proposed to on the side of a road!" He dropped his head.

"There's nothing wrong with roads. They lead up mountains." She remembered Paolo's clay model of the embracing couple morphing into a mountain. Love as a mountain. She wanted to climb this mountain with him. "Yes, Paolo, I'll be your wife."

CHAPTER 46

Alice checked one last time that her wallet, phone and passport were in her backpack. It felt like eons ago when Rachel suggested that she might be eligible for an Italian passport. Little did either of them know, back then, that she would get so much more than a passport: love, family and connections.

Paolo's family had welcomed her like one of their own and had loved her even after discovering that her relationship with Paolo was fake. They had all worked to help the pretence turn into reality.

At breakfast, Paolo had announced that they were going to get married. Agostino had clapped and Vittoria and Agatina had whooped and cheered. It had taken a lot of effort to stop Lia ringing Marcello and Rosaria at eight o'clock in the morning during their honeymoon to share the news.

The whole village had been invited to an impromptu lunch to celebrate their engagement. This time, when Agostino got out the bottles of bubbly, Alice was ready for the public kiss.

Now their cases were in the car with Agostino who was ready to drive them to the airport.

"I'll come visit you," Vittoria told Alice.

"You never came to visit me!" Paolo said with mock resentment.

"That would have been boring."

Lia came in the car with them. As they drove away from Altavicia, Alice felt that this place was like a home and

Paolo's family was her family, too.

The first thing she would do when she got home was sign up for Italian language classes.

At the airport's departures hall she found a little surprise.

A couple wearing dark glasses and the kind of wide-brimmed hats that paparazzi hate were waiting for her.

"I know we said goodbye but we wanted to see you one more time," Luigi told her.

"Keep in touch," Simona said.

"I will," Alice replied.

"If you can't get hold of me because I'm on tour, leave a message for me with Simona," Luigi urged.

Alice smiled. It was wonderful that the teen lovers were finally reunited. And what a privilege to have been instrumental to their reunion!

As she and Paolo walked through to Departures and waved back at their respective parents, Alice wondered if she would ever call Simona and Luigi "Mamma" and "Papà". But even if she never did, they were now family to her. And if her adoptive parents were looking down from above, they were surely proud of what she had done.

The End

OTHER BOOKS BY STEFANIA HARTLEY

Other Books in this Series

Sweet Competition for Camillo's Café

Camillo runs a popular café on Altavicia's main square. Giada runs an equally popular café across the square. They have both entered Altavicia's Best Café competition.

Scarred by his father's death, Camillo's greatest wish is to escape the Calabrian seaside village and return to his beloved London, where his family was last together and happy. Abandoned by her parents, Giada's greatest wish is to earn her nonna's love. The competition trophy is the ticket to both their dreams, but only one can win.

As Camillo discovers that happiness doesn't come from a location and Giada that love isn't earned, can enemies become friends, and maybe more?

Collections of short stories

Welcome to Quayside

Forty-year-old Tanya Baker dreams of starting a new life and making friends when she moves to a block of flats by the River Thames with her thirteen-year-old daughter, Hattie. But as Tanya and Hattie knock on neighbours' door in search of a tin opener, it's clear that the residents of Number One Quayside like to keep to themselves. Everyone, that is, except their next-door neighbours, Italian chef Giacomo Dalamo, and his thirteen-year-old daughter, Frankie. Between a delicious dish of lasagne (Giacomo's) and a burnt salad (Tanya's), they hatch a plan to set a library of things in their building, so that residents can borrow rarely-used items, from DIY tools to sports equipment and party supplies. First, though, Tanya and Giacomo must win over their neighbours, persuade the building's management company, source library stock by kayaking down the Thames, and deal with plumbing disasters, all the while trying to protect their bruised hearts from falling for each other.

Stars Are Silver

Is it too late for Melina to learn to drive? Is Don Pericle's vow never to fall in love again still valid after fifty years? Will a falling piano squash

Filomena or just shake up her heart? Why does the mother of the bride ask Don Pericle to cancel the wedding?

Fresh from the Sea

Will Gnà Peppina give her customers what they need, even if it's more than food? What pleasures can a man indulge in after his wife has put him on a draconian diet? Who will be able to cook dinner for the family with five euros?

Confetti and Lemon Blossom

For Don Pericle, wedding organising is a calling, not just a career. Deep in the Sicilian countryside, between rose gardens and trellised balconies, up marble staircases and across damasked ballrooms, these charming stories unfold: stories of star-crossed love, of comedic misunderstandings and of deep friendships, of love triumphing in the face of adversity.

A Slip of the Tongue

Will Melina regret faking to be sick to avoid her chores? Can Don Pericle organise a wedding for a groom who doesn't know? Who has stolen the marble pisces from the cathedral's floor?

What's Yours is Mine

Can Melina give away her husband's possessions because they've always said that 'what's mine is yours and what's yours is mine'? Will the 'Sleep Doctor' deliver on his promises? How will the young Sicilian duke, Pericle, help his friend get married?

Tales from the Parish

Father Okoli dreams of owning a flock of hens and studying for a PhD, when his bishop saddles him with yet another parish to look after.

But as Father moves to Moreton-on-the-Edge, a farming village in the English Cotswolds, he's plugged into a community of warm-hearted characters, from the motherly parish secretary to her septuagenarian neighbour who's become a cycling champion, and from teenagers requiring driving lessons to atheist publicans who believe in miracles.

As the community pulls together to reopen the village's Electric Picture House, dreams are fulfilled, teen love blossoms and Father Okoli feels that Moreton-on-the-Edge is now home.

A Season of Goodwill

How far should Viviana's family go to avoid being thirteen at the table? Should Melina and Tanino attend a New Year's party hosted by Melina's old flame? Why do Don Pericle's clients want a Christmas wedding at all costs?

Drive Me Crazy

"Cohabitation is tribulation" goes an

Italian saying, and after more than fifty years of married life, Tanino and Melina know a thing or two about the challenges of living together.
Follow their antics in this collection of twelve short stories dedicated entirely to the much-loved Sicilian couple.

ABOUT THE AUTHOR

Stefania was born in Sicily and immediately started growing, but not very much.

She left her sunny island after falling head over heels in love with an Englishman, and now she lives in the UK with her husband and their three children.

Having finally learnt English, she's enjoying it so much that she now writes short stories and romance novels. Her short stories have been longlisted for the Mogford Prize for Food and Drink Writing, commended by the Society of Medical Authors, and won other prizes.

If you have enjoyed these stories, please consider leaving a review.

If you want to hear when she's releasing a new book, sign up for the newsletter at:

www.stefaniahartley.com/ subscribe You'll also receive an exclusive short story.